May 12

THE CAT WHO ROBBED A BANK

Also by Lilian Jackson Braun

LILIAN JACKSON BRAUN

THE
CAT WHO
ROBBED A BANK

G . P . PUTNAM'S SONS

NEW YORK

Bra

This is a work of fiction. Names, characters, places, and
incidents either are the product of the author's imagination
or are used fictitiously, and any resemblance to actual
persons living or dead, business establishments, events,
or locales is entirely coincidental.

G. P. Putnam's Sons
Publishers Since 1838
a member of
Penguin Putnam Inc.
375 Hudson Street
New York, NY 10014

Library of Congress Cataloging-in-Publication Data

Braun, Lilian Jackson.
The cat who robbed a bank / Lilian Jackson Braun.
p.   cm.
ISBN 0-399-14570-2
I. Title.
PS3552.R354 C348   1999   99-32581 CIP
813'.54—dc21

Printed in the United States of America

1   3   5   7   9   10   8   6   4   2

This book is printed on acid-free paper. ∞

Book design by Patrice Sheridan

DEDICATED TO EARL BETTINGER,
THE HUSBAND WHO . . .

THE CAT WHO ROBBED A BANK

one

It was a September to remember! In Moose County, 400 miles north of everywhere, plans were rife and hopes were high.

First, the historic hotel in Pickax City, the county seat, was finally restored after the bombing of the previous year, and it would reopen with a new name, a new chef, and a gala reception.

Then, a famous American (who may or may not have slept there in 1895) was about to be honored with the city's first annual Mark Twain Festival.

Next, a distinguished personage from Chicago had reserved the presidential suite and would arrive on Labor Day, setting female hearts aflutter.

To top it off, the tri-county Scottish Gathering and Highland Games would be held at the fairgrounds: bagpipes skirling, strong men in kilts tossing the caber, and pretty young women dancing the Highland Fling on the balls of their feet.

The one unexpected happening was the homicide on

the Pickax police blotter, but that was a long story, starting twenty-odd years before.

As September approached, the good folk of Pickax (population 3,000) were quoting Mark Twain about the weather, suggesting ribald names for the hotel, and gossiping endlessly about a man named Delacamp; few would ever meet him, but all had something to say about him.

Jim Qwilleran, columnist for the *Moose County Something*, felt an air of anticipation when he made his rounds of downtown Pickax. When he went to the bank to cash a check, the young woman who counted out his fifties said, "Isn't it exciting? Mr. Delacamp is coming again, and he always comes into the bank. I hope he comes to my window, but the manager usually handles his transactions. Anyway, it's all so thrilling!"

"If you say so," Qwilleran said. After a long career as a newspaperman he was seldom excited and certainly never thrilled.

At the florist shop where he went to order a flowering plant for a sick friend, the wide-eyed assistant said breathlessly, "Did you hear? Mr. Delacamp is coming! He always has to have fresh flowers in his hotel room, and he sends roses to his customers."

"Good!" said Qwilleran. "Anything that helps the local economy has my approval."

While picking up a *New York Times* at the drugstore he heard a woman customer saying she had received an engraved invitation to Mr. Delacamp's afternoon tea, and she wondered what kind of perfume to wear. The pharmacist's wife said, "They say he likes French perfumes.

We don't carry anything like that. Try the department store. They can special-order."

Qwilleran crossed the street to the department store, his newshound instincts scenting a good story with human interest and a touch of humor. Lanspeak's was a large fourth-generation store with new-fashioned merchandise but old-fashioned ideas about customer service. He found the two owners in their cramped office on the main floor.

"Hi, Qwill! Come on in!" said Larry Lanspeak.

"Have a cup of coffee," said his wife, Carol.

Qwilleran took a chair. "No coffee, thanks, but please tell me something. Explain the Delacamp mystique." He knew the couple were official hosts for the man's visit. "Why all the excitement?"

Larry looked at his wife, and she made a helpless gesture. "What can I say? He's an older man, but he's handsome elegant—gallant! He sends women roses!"

"And kisses their hands," said Larry with raised eyebrows.

"He pays lavish compliments!"

"And kisses hands," Larry repeated derisively.

"Everything is very formal. Women have to wear hats to his Tuesday afternoon tea, and we've sold out of millinery. We sell the basic felt that women wear to church, but our daughter said we should gussy them up with feathers and flowers and huge ribbon bows. So we did! Diane is a sober, dedicated M.D., but she has a mad streak."

"Takes after her mother," Larry said.

"The results are really wild! Sorry you can't write it up,

Qwill, but everything is private, invitational, and exclusive. No publicity!"

"Okay. I'll forget it. No story," Qwilleran acquiesced. "But he sounds like an interesting character . . . You two go back to work."

Larry accompanied him out of the office and toward the front door, down the main aisle between cases of men's shirts and ties and women's scarves and earrings. "Old Campo is harmless, although a trifle phony," he said. "Still, his visits every four or five years are good for a certain element in our community—and good public relations for the store. It's Carol's project, actually. I stay out of it."

The facts were that Delacamp was a dealer who bought and sold estate jewelry, making periodic visits to remote areas with a history of affluence. In such communities the descendants of old moneyed families might be willing to part with an heirloom necklace of rubies and emeralds, or a diamond tiara, in order to finance a new car or a college education or an extravagant cruise. Artisans in Delacamp's Chicago firm could break up such outdated items and re-mount them in rings, pendants, earrings, and so forth for sale to a new generation—as an investment or status symbol.

Moose County fitted the picture, and Delacamp apparently had found his visits worthwhile. It had been the richest county in the state in the nineteenth century, when natural resources were being exploited and there was no income tax to pay. The old mining tycoons and lumber barons had built themselves mansions with large vaults in the basement. They had sent their offspring to eastern colleges and had taken their wives to Paris, where they bought them jewels that would appreciate in value. When the mines closed in the early twentieth century, the economy collapsed and most families fled to the big cities. Others elected to stay and live quietly on their private means, going into business or the professions—or even bootlegging during Prohibition.

All of this convinced Qwilleran that Old Campo had a good thing going, and he enjoyed listening to gossip in the coffee shops. Blue-collar and white-collar opinions were freely expressed:

"He'll be puttin' on the dog and gettin' the old gals all het up."

"They say he drinks nothin' but tea, but ten to one he puts a little somethin' in it."

"Yeah, I was night porter at the hotel a few years ago, and he used to send out for rum. He was a big tipper, I'll say that for him."

"I know a guy—his wife drew ten thousand from their joint account and bought a diamond pin."

"I'm glad my wife's not on his list. Women go to that tea party of his and they're pushovers!"

"He always brings a female assistant, and she always happens to be young and sexy. She's supposed to be his cousin or niece or something, but you never notice any family resemblance, if you know what I mean."

Gossip was the mainstay of Moose County culture, although it was called "caring and sharing." Men had their coffee shops; women had their afternoon circles.

Qwilleran listened to it and nodded and chuckled. He himself had been the subject of gossip. He was a bachelor who lived simply, and yet he was the richest man in the northeast central United States. Through a twist of fate he had fallen heir to the vast Klingenschoen fortune based in Moose County. Previously he had managed on a reporter's salary without any particular interest in wealth; in financial matters, moreover, he felt like a simpleton. He handled the situation by establishing the Klingenschoen Foundation with a mandate to give the money away judiciously to benefit the community.

Needless to say, "Mr. Q" had become an icon in the north country, not only because of his generosity. He wrote a twice-weekly column, "Straight from the Qwill Pen," that was the most popular feature in the newspaper. He had a genial disposition and a sense of humor, even though his brooding eyes gave him a look of melancholy. And he was his own man.

Pioneer blood had made the natives into a race of determined individualists, as a glance at the map would confirm. There were places like Squunk Corners, Little Hope, Sawdust City, Chipmunk, and Ugley Gardens. Qwilleran belonged in this environment. He spelled his name with a QW, lived in a barn with two cats, sported an enormous pepper-and-salt moustache, and rode a recumbent bicycle which required him to pedal with feet elevated.

There were other characteristics in his favor. Being tall and well-built, he had a distinct aura of authority. Being a journalist, he had trained himself to listen. Strangers felt they could confide in him, air their dreams, relate their woes. He always listened sympathetically.

One of Qwilleran's quirks was his desire for privacy.

He needed solitude for thinking, writing, and reading, and his converted barn was effectively secluded. Though within the city limits and not far from Main Street, it had acreage. It had once been a strip farm extending from Main Street to Trevelyan Road, which was a half-mile to the east. Paving was unknown in those days.

Now Main Street divided into northbound and south-bound traffic lanes, called Park Circle. Around the rim were two churches, the courthouse, a majestic old public library, and the original Klingenschoen mansion, now functioning as a small theatre for stage productions. To the rear of the mansion was a four-stall carriage house with servants' quarters upstairs. From there a rustic wagon trail wound its way through evergreen woods, ending in a barnyard.

The hundred-year-old apple barn rose like an ancient castle—octagonal in design, four stories high, with a fieldstone foundation and siding of weathered shingles. Odd-shaped windows had been cut in the walls, reflecting the angled timbers that framed the interior.

The property to the east had been a thriving orchard until a mysterious blight struck the trees. Now it was re-forested, and wild gardens attracted birds and butterflies.

On the last day of August Qwilleran walked down the old orchard lane to pick up his mail and newspaper on Trevelyan Road. On the site where the old farmhouse had burned down there was now a rustic contemporary building housing the Pickax Art Center. County residents attended classes there, viewed exhibitions, and—in some cases—rented studios. As Qwilleran passed it, he counted the cars in the parking lot. It looked as if they were having a good day.

The highway marked the city limits. Beyond it was farmland. He waved to a farmer chugging down the road on a tractor and the driver of a farm truck traveling in the opposite direction. His rural mailbox and a newspaper sleeve were mounted on posts alongside the pavement. There were few letters in the box; his fan mail went to the newspaper office, and official business and junk mail went to the law firm that represented the Klingenschoen Foundation.

A boy carrying a grocery sack was running toward him from the direction of the McBee farm. "Mr. Q! Mr. Q!" he shouted. It was the ten-year-old Culvert McBee. "I brought you something!"

Qwilleran hoped it was not turnips or parsnips from the McBee kitchen garden. "That's very good of you, Culvert."

The chubby boy was breathing hard after running. "I made something for you . . . I took a summer class . . . over there." He jerked his head toward the art center and then handed over the sack.

"What is it?"

"Look inside."

Qwilleran was dubious about knickknacks made for him by fond readers, and he peered into the sack with no great expectations. What he saw was a pad of paper stapled on a small board. The top sheet was computer-printed with the well-known saying *Thirty Days Hath September*.

"It's a calendar," Culvert explained. "Every day you tear off a page and read what it says."

The second page had the date (September 1) and the day (Tuesday) and a brief saying: *Let sleeping dogs lie*.

"Well! This is really something!" Qwilleran said with a good show of enthusiasm. He flipped through the pages and read: *What's good for the goose is good for the gander . . . You can lead a horse to water but you can't make him drink . . . A cat can look at a king.* "Where did you get these sayings, Culvert?"

"At the library. They're from all over the world."

"They're all about animals!"

"Yep."

"Well, I certainly appreciate your thoughtfulness!"

"There's a hole in the board. You can hang it on a nail."

"I'll do that."

"I made one for my mom, too."

"How are your parents? I haven't seen them lately."

"Dad's okay. Mom has a sore hand from using the computer."

"How about the dogs?" Culvert had a shelter for old, unwanted dogs.

"Dolly died of old age and I buried her behind the shed. I painted her name on a stone. You can come and look at it if you want to. My aunt came and brought flowers."

"That was nice of her. Are you ready to go back to school?"

"Yep."

Then Qwilleran praised the calendar once more, and Culvert walked back to his farm on Base Line Road.

. . .

At the art center there was a familiar car parked on the lot, and Qwilleran went in to talk with his friend, Thornton Haggis. He was a retiree with a shock of white hair, now serving as interim manager until they could find a replacement for Beverly Forfar.

"Still holding the fort, I see," Qwilleran said. "Has anyone heard from Bev?"

"No. After the turmoil she experienced here, I believe she was glad to wash her hands of our fair city."

The former manager had written to Qwilleran, however, thanking him profusely for his farewell gift, little knowing it was something he had been trying to unload.

She had written, "It was so wonderful of you to arrange for me to have *The Whiteness of White*. It hangs in my apartment, where it is admired by everyone. You may be interested to know I have found a small job in Ann Arbor, Michigan, that could develop into something big."

Qwilleran nodded. From what he knew of that city it had the right climate for an esoteric intaglio. He had won it in a raffle at the art center, simply because he was the only one who bought a chance. He bought several, using the alias of Ronald Frobnitz. As the winner he was trying to dispose of it discreetly without offending the artist who had donated it. Luckily Beverly Forfar was leaving Pickax forever, and she was happy to acquire an artwork valued at a thousand dollars.

In a postscript to her letter she had written, "If you are in touch with Professor Frobnitz in Japan, please thank him for his generosity. I'm sorry I didn't meet him while he was in Pickax. On the telephone he sounded positively charming."

Qwilleran asked Thornton, "Any good prospects for Beverly's successor?"

"They've interviewed a few applicants but can't seem to make a decision."

"You're doing too good a job, Thorn. Why hire a manager when good old Thorn will do the work free?"

"Don't think that hasn't crossed my mind! After September thirtieth, I quit! Meanwhile we're setting up the craft fair. Are you coming to the opening? I'll have a few of my own things on exhibit."

"Are you doing something creative in tombstones?" Qwilleran asked lightly.

Thornton was a retired stonecutter who had studied art history at one time. "You can kid all you like," he retorted, "but I felt the need for a manual hobby. I bought a lathe, and now I'm doing woodturning in my basement."

"That I've got to see!" Qwilleran said.

"Then come to the craft fair," his friend said. "Bring money."

When Qwilleran walked up the lane to the apple barn, he was approaching from the east. In its heyday it had been a drive-through barn with huge doors east and west, large enough to admit a horse-drawn wagon loaded with apples. Now the huge openings had been filled in and equipped with human-size doors. On the east side there were handsome double doors flanked by glass panels. These were the front doors, opening into the foyer, although they were on the back of the building. The back door was, of course, on the front, opening into the kitchen. (This kind of anomaly was common in Moose

County, where Pickax was referred to as Paradox.) Twice
the Pickax voters had vetoed a proposal to change the
names of streets. "Old East Street" was west of "New
West Street," and there was confusion about "North
Street East" and "South Street West." Only strangers were
befuddled, however, and befuddling strangers was a local
pastime.

As Qwilleran approached the double doors, two Siamese cats watched from the sidelights, standing on their
hindlegs with their forepaws on the low windowsill. Entering the foyer he had to wade through weaving bodies
and waving tails, circling him, doubling back, rubbing
his ankles, and getting under his feet—all the while yowling in the operatic voices of Siamese. The tumultuous
welcome would have been flattering if Qwilleran had not
consulted his watch. It was feeding time at the zoo!

"What have you guys been doing this afternoon?" he
asked as he prepared their dinner. "Anything worthwhile? Solve any world problems? Who won the fifty-
yard dash?" The more you talk to cats, the smarter they
become, he believed.

The long, lean, lithe muscular one was Kao K'o Kung,
familiarly known as Koko. His female companion was
Yum Yum—small, dainty, shy, although she could shriek
like an ambulance siren when she wanted something and
wanted it immediately. Both had pale fawn-colored fur
and seal brown masks, ears and tails. Her eyes were blue
tinged with violet, and their appealing kittenish gaze
could break hearts. Koko's deeper blue eyes had a depth
that suggested secret intelligence and untold mysteries.

They were indoor cats, but the barn interior was as big
as all outdoors to a small creature weighing ten pounds or

less. The space, a hundred feet in diameter, was open to the roof. A ramp spiraled up the walls and connected the balconies on three levels. In the center stood a huge white fireplace cube with white stacks soaring to the cupola, and it divided the main floor into functional areas: dining, lounging, foyer, and library. The kitchen was under a balcony, half hidden by an L-shaped snack bar.

In the daytime a flood of light came through triangles and rhomboids of glass. Pale colors prevailed—in the bleached timbers, upholstered furniture, and Moroccan rugs. After dark, when a single switch activated indirect lights and artfully placed spotlights, the effect was nothing less than enchanting.

Qwilleran's favorite haunt was the library area. One wall of the fireplace cube was covered with bookshelves, and the shelves were filled with secondhand classics purchased from a local bookseller. A library table held the telephone, answering machine, and writing materials. In a capacious lounge chair with an ottoman Qwilleran liked to read aloud to the Siamese or draft his column on a legal pad with a soft lead pencil.

On the last day of August, before going out to dinner, he read to the cats from a book selected by Koko. He was the official bibliocat. He prowled the bookshelves and liked to curl up between the biographies and the nineteenth-century English fiction. At reading time it was his privilege to select the title, although Qwilleran had the power of veto. They had been reading Greek drama. Koko could sense which book was which, and he repeatedly sniffed *The Frogs* by Aristophanes.

"Okay, we'll do it once more," Qwilleran said, "but

this is the last time!" Both cats liked the froggy chorus that he dramatized so colorfully: *brekekekex koax koax*. Yum Yum's eyes grew wide, and a rumble came from Koko's chest.

"Those cats are just like little kids," Qwilleran said at dinner that night. "When I was three years old, I wanted to hear *Jack and the Beanstalk* over and over again. It was in desperation that my mother taught me to read so young."

He was dining with the chief woman in his life, a charming companion of his own age, whose gentle voice, soft smile, and agreeable disposition camouflaged a will as strong as Yum Yum's. She was Polly Duncan, director of the public library. She always wore something special for their dates, and this time it was a green silk dress with a necklace of long slivers of silver alternating with beads of green jade.

"You look lovely!" he said. He had learned not to say, "You look lovely *tonight*." That would imply that she usually looked unlovely. Polly was sensitive about the niceties of speech.

Pleased, she said, "Thank you, dear. And you're look-ing very handsome!"

He always wore a coat and tie, well coordinated, when having dinner with Polly. It was a compliment they paid each other.

They had a reservation at Onoosh's in downtown Pickax, a café with the exotic murals, lamps, brasses, and aromas of the Mediterranean rim. Ethnic foods were fi-nally being accepted 400 miles north of everywhere, although it had been a slow process. Seated at the brass-topped tables were foodists with adventurous palates, vacationers from out of town, and students from Moose County Community College, who were eligible for a discount.

For starters Polly had a dry sherry and Qwilleran ordered Squunk water on the rocks with a twist, a local mineral water.

"What's the latest gossip at the library?" he asked. It was a center of information in more ways than one. "Has the Pickax grapevine blown a gasket over Mr. Delacamp?"

"No, no!" she corrected him with excitement. "The latest news is about Amanda! Haven't you heard?"

"I heard the rumor in July, while you were in Canada, but she denied it."

"She changed her mind several times after that, but I think she was building up suspense. There's nothing naive about Amanda!"

"So what's the latest?" he asked impatiently. As a journalist he always felt uncomfortable if he didn't know the latest.

"Well! Today was the deadline, and she picked up her petition at city hall at nine A.M. Eight hours later, she returned it with the required number of signatures—five percent of registered voters! She stood in front of Toodle's Market and Lanspeak's and created quite a stir, as you can well imagine."

"That's our Amanda!" Qwilleran gloated.

There was only one illustrious Amanda in Pickax. As owner of the design studio on Main Street she had decorated the homes of well-known families for forty years.

She had served on the city council for twenty years—always outspoken and sometimes cantankerous. The locals loved her for her fearless individualism, and that included her eccentric dress and grooming. Now she was daring to challenge the incumbent mayor in the November election—a politician who had held office for five terms, simply because his mother was a Goodwinter.

That was the big name in Pickax. The four Goodwinter brothers had founded the city in 1850.

But the mayor's name was Gregory Blythe. His challenger was Amanda *Goodwinter!*

Qwilleran said, "I predict she'll win by a landslide."

A bright young woman in an embroidered vest served them baba ghanouj and spanokopetes, and he said, "I wish my mother could see me now—eating spinach and eggplant. And liking it!" Then he asked, "What's the latest on Old Campo?"

"How can you be so derisive?" Polly rebuked him. "The jealousy among our male population is ludicrous! A few members of my library board are on his guest list, and they say he's a grand gentleman with polished manners and great charisma!"

"I hear he always has a girl Friday who travels with him and happens to be young, sexy, and related by blood." He said this with an ounce of sarcasm.

Polly replied in all seriousness, "He's training family members to take over the business when he retires. . . . Or so I'm told," she added. "But the big news is that Carol has asked me to pour at his celebrated Tuesday Tea! Those opals you gave me were ordered by Carol from a Chicago jeweler. That was Delacamp's firm, and so I'm suddenly in the inner circle."

"Just what does he do when he's in town?"

"Well, first he gives an exclusive tea for potential customers. Then families with heirloom jewelry to sell invite him to their homes, and those who wish to buy vintage jewelry from his private collection make appointments to meet him in his hotel suite."

Qwilleran considered the situation briefly and then asked, "If he's so discriminating, how did he react to the old hotel with its broken-down elevators and wretched food?"

"He had the good taste not to criticize or make fun of it. . . . I don't mind telling you, Qwill: I'm having stage fright about pouring tea for him."

"Nonsense, Polly. You're always in control, and now that you've had your surgery, you're healthier and livelier and more admirable than ever."

The young waitress serving the entrees grinned to see "an older couple" holding hands across the table.

"Don't snicker," Qwilleran told her. "It's an old Mediterranean custom."

For a few moments they contemplated the presentation of food on the plate—stuffed grape leaves for her, curried lamb for him—and the subtlety of the flavors. Then he asked, "What are you wearing to the reception Saturday night?"

"My white dinner dress and the opals. Are you wearing your kilt with your dinner jacket?"

"I think it would be appropriate."

The grand opening of the refurbished hotel would be a black-tie event at three hundred dollars a ticket, proceeds going to Moose County's Literacy Council. There would be champagne, music, and a preview of the renovated facility.

Qwilleran said, "I'm getting a preview of the preview. Fran Brodie is sneaking me in."

"It was a stroke of genius to rename the hotel, considering its grim reputation in the past."

"The new sign is going up Thursday."

Conversation lapsed into trivia:

The theatre club was opening its season with *Night Must Fall*.

The art center had been unable to replace Beverly Forfar.

Celia Robinson had married Pat O'Dell and had moved into his big house on Pleasant Street, leaving the carriage-house apartment vacant.

When finally they left the restaurant, Qwilleran asked, "Would you like to stop at the barn and see my new calendar?"

"For just a minute. I have to go home and feed the cats."

It was twilight when they drove into the barnyard. A faint, dusky blue light seemed to bathe the world. It was the breathless moment after sunset and before the stars appeared, when all is silent . . . waiting.

"Magical," Polly said.

"The French have a word for it: l'heure bleue."

"There's a French perfume by that name. I imagine it's lovely."

Eventually they went indoors to look at the calendar, and eventually Polly went home to feed Brutus and Catta. Qwilleran took the Siamese out to the screened gazebo, and the three of them sat in the dark. The cats liked the nighttime. They heard inaudible sounds and saw invisible movement in the shadows.

Suddenly Koko was alert. He ran to the rear of the gazebo and stared at the barn. In two or three minutes the phone rang indoors. Qwilleran hurried back to the main building and grabbed the receiver after the sixth or seventh ring.

The caller was Celia Robinson O'Dell, who had been his neighbor in the carriage-house apartment. "Hi, Chief!" she said cheerfully, her voice sounding young for a woman of her advancing age. "How's everything at the barn? How are the kitties?"

"Celia! I've been trying to call you and extend felicitations on your marriage, but you're hard to reach."

"We took a little honeymoon trip. We went to see Pat's married daughter in Green Bay. He has three grand-children."

"How do you like living on Pleasant Street?"

"Oh, it's a wonderful big house with a big kitchen, which I need now that I'm going into the catering business seriously. But I enjoyed living in the carriage house and running over with goodies for you and the kitties. I can still cook a few things for your freezer, you know, and Pat can deliver them when he does your yardwork."

"That'll be much appreciated by all three of us."

"And if there are any little . . . secret . . . missions that I can handle for you . . ."

"Well, we'll see how that works out. Give Pat my congratulations. He's a lucky guy."

As Qwilleran hung up the phone, he stroked his moustache dubiously, fearing that his espionage stratagem was collapsing. He liked to snoop in matters that were none of his business—propelled by curiosity or suspicion—and he had relied on Celia to preserve his anonymity. She was an ideal undercover agent, being a respectable, trustworthy, grandmotherly type. And, as an avid reader of spy fiction, she enjoyed being assigned to covert missions. There had been briefings, cryptic phone calls, hidden tape recorders, and secret meetings in the produce department at Toodle's Market. Now, as a married woman, how long could she retain her cover?

As for Qwilleran, there was nothing official about his investigations. He simply had an interest in crime, stemming from his years as a crime reporter for newspapers Down Below—as locals called the metropolitan areas to the south. In recent years he had uncovered plenty of intrigue in this small community, and in doing so he had won the trust and friendship of the Pickax police chief. It was an association that would continue, with or without his secret agent.

two

Tuesday, September 1—*Let sleeping dogs lie.*

Qwilleran had written a thousand words in praise of September for the "Qwill Pen" column, and he invited readers to compose poems about the ninth month. He wrote, "The best will be printed in the 'Qwill Pen' and will win a Qwill pencil, stamped in gold." Everyone knew that his favorite writing tool was a fat yellow pencil with thick soft lead.

"Always figuring out ways to get the subscribers to do your work for you," the managing editor bantered.

"Reader participation is the name of the game. They love it!"

"Who's paying for all the pencils you're giving away?"

"You can take it out of my meager salary."

WEDNESDAY, SEPTEMBER 2—*Don't count your chickens before they're hatched.*

The weekly luncheon of the Pickax Boosters Club was held at the community hall, with committees reporting on the progress of the Mark Twain Festival, scheduled for October. There would be a parade, a square dance, contests, lectures, and more. The so-called presidential suite in the hotel (third floor front) would be renamed the Mark Twain suite. Efforts to name a street after him had received a chilly reaction from residents, who complained that a change in street names resulted only in confusion and expense to property owners. Qwilleran attended and ate his soup and sandwich but refrained from volunteering for anything.

THURSDAY, SEPTEMBER 3—*Every dog has his day.*

For the Siamese the big event was the arrival of a truck delivering new stools for the snack bar. The old ones were as comfortable as a milking stool, yet casual visitors chose to sit there instead of sinking into the deep-cushioned lounge chairs. The new stools were more hospitable. They had backs; they swiveled; their seats were thickly upholstered. The four old stools without backs would go to the thrift shop to be sold for charity.

As soon as the deliveryman had left, Koko and Yum Yum came out from nowhere to inspect the new furniture. Two noses covered every inch of the wooden legs and backs; then they curled up on two upholstered seats and went to sleep.

Fran Brodie had ordered them. She was second-in-command at Amanda's interior design studio. She was also the daughter of the police chief and one of the most glamorous young women in town. And on Friday she would be giving Qwilleran a personally conducted tour of the refurbished hotel.

FRIDAY, SEPTEMBER 4—*A short horse is soon curried.*

Qwilleran fed the cats, changed the water in their drinking bowl, policed their commode, brushed their coats, and gave them instructions for the day: "Don't forget to wash behind your ears. Drink plenty of water; it's good for you. Be nice to each other."

They looked at him blankly and waited for him to leave so they could enjoy a nap on the new bar stools.

For his own breakfast he thawed a roll and took it to his studio on the first balcony, along with a mug of extra-strength coffee brewed in his automated coffeemaker. There he finished his Friday column, a tongue-in-cheek dissertation on the advantages and disadvantages of indoor plumbing. Only Qwilleran could write a thousand words on a subject of such delicacy and make it entertaining—as well as educational—without being scatological.

He handed in his copy to a skeptical managing editor, bantered with the crew in the cityroom, grabbed a burger at Lois's Luncheonette, and browsed among the preowned books in the dusty secondhand bookstore. Still he arrived early at the hotel for his appointment with the designer.

After the bombing of the historic building, the Klingenschoen Foundation had purchased it from the Limburger estate, and Qwilleran had insisted that a local designer be commissioned to do the interior. Now, while waiting for Fran Brodie, he stood on the sidewalk across the street and contemplated the scene. The three blocks of downtown Main Street reflected an era when the county's quarries were going full blast. Buildings and pavement were made of stone—a bleak prospect until the city's recent beautification effort. Now the chipped flagstone pavements were replaced with brick. Young trees were planted close to the curb. Brick planter boxes were filled with petunias, tended by volunteers.

In the middle of the block stood the three-story cube of granite that had long been the city's only hotel and most disgraceful eyesore. It had a long history: built in the 1870s . . . gutted by fire in the 1920s and cheaply rebuilt . . . known as an overnight lodging that was gloomy but clean!

"It was so clean," said the natives, "that the porcelain was scrubbed off the bathtubs!"

After being bombed by a psychopath from Down Below, it required a year to rebuild, refurnish and rename. Already two national magazines were interested in photographing the interior.

Windows that had previously stared balefully on Main Street were now flanked by wooden shutters painted in the theme color of rust. The entrance was more inviting than before; a broad flight of stone steps led up to double doors of beveled wood and etched glass. And across the facade were stainless steel letters mounted directly on the stone. They spelled:

THE MACKINTOSH INN

As everyone in Moose County knew, Qwilleran's mother had been a Mackintosh. If she had not been a wartime volunteer, and if she had not met Francesca Klingenschoen in a canteen, and if they had not become lifelong friends . . . there would be no Mackintosh Inn. As a boy he had written letters to "Aunt Fanny." After his mother's death and numerous crises in his own life, he resumed the correspondence and eventually found himself named as her sole heir.

Qwilleran's reverie was interrupted by a pinch on the elbow and the sound of a woman's well-modulated voice: "Well, what do you think of the old dump?"

He gulped involuntarily. "Fran, I wish my mother could see this."

"Wait till you see the interior!"

They dashed across the street during a lull in the traffic, and as they stood at the foot of the broad front steps she explained, "This is the ceremonial entrance. In the rear we have a carriage entrance at ground level, close to the parking lot and with immediate access to the elevators."

"Elevators? Plural?" he asked in pleasure and surprise.

"Two of them. They operate like a dream! No clanking, no jerking, no stopping between floors. Isn't it wonderful? . . . Now, before we go inside, I want to brief you on a couple of details. The interior is done in the Arts & Crafts period. Do you know about that?"

"Vaguely. Tell me."

It came after Victorian and before Art Deco. In England the leader was William Morris . . . in Scotland, Charles Rennie Mackintosh . . . in the U.S., Gustav Stickley. Their designs are in museums and private collections. We've furnished the inn with new versions of historic originals. . . . Got it?"

"Got it. Let's go." As they walked slowly up the steps he gazed at the entrance doors in admiration. "Old?"

"No. Custom-made for us in North Carolina. The wood is fumed oak. The etching was inspired by a William Morris tapestry."

In the lobby Qwilleran, who was not prone to gasp, actually gasped! The mood was hospitable, the colors warm: rust, mellow browns, and other earth tones. There was much fumed oak . . . ceiling beams where none had been before . . . large leather-cushioned chairs with wide wood arms . . . tables with ceramic tile tops . . . lamps with wood bases, pyramidal shades of mica, and pull chains! The mica gave a golden glow. The new reception desk had a welcoming air.

"The old one," Qwilleran observed, "resembled the booking desk at the police station." Then he saw the large oil painting on the far wall: a life-size portrait of a woman seated at a piano. "*That's her!* That's exactly how she looked!"

It was a portrait of Anne Mackintosh Qwilleran in a peach-colored dress. Paul Skumble, the portraitist from Lockmaster who refused to copy photographs, had painted her likeness from Qwilleran's memories: "People said she looked like Greer Garson but with larger eyes . . . Her hair was brown and medium-length; she called it a pageboy . . . Her hands looked slender and fragile at the keyboard; she had a baby grand . . . I remember a peach-colored dress with pearl buttons down the front, and a bracelet with foreign coins dangling from it."

From this sketchy description the artist had created an astounding likeness complete with bracelet. And he had gone to the trouble of finding a video of an old Greer Garson movie.

Qwilleran said to Fran, "Actually she never wore the bracelet while playing the piano. It jangled. But we won't tell anyone."

"She has a gracious aristocratic look."

"True, but I didn't think of it in those terms when I was a kid. I just thought it was motherliness—a kind of calm, fond assurance that 'mother knows best.'. . . I have to phone Paul and congratulate him."

"Wait till tomorrow," she suggested. "He's coming to the reception."

"In his usual ragged jeans and paint-spattered T-shirt?"

"*Please!* I personally dragged him to Bruce's Tuxedo Rental and talked him into trimming his beard—just a trifle, not enough to crush his personality. . . . Are you ready to see the rest of the building?"

The dining room was now the Mackintosh Room—with white tablecloths and black-lacquered Stickley chairs. They had square-spindled backs and upholstered seats covered in the Mackintosh tartan. That was red, with a dark green stripe, and the carpet was dark green. The focal point on the back wall was a large Mackintosh crest in wrought iron, said to come from a Scottish castle gate. It had a cat rampant and the clan motto: *Touch not the cat bott a glove*.

The coffee shop was now called Rennie's and was done in the style of a Glasgow tea room designed by Charles Rennie Mackintosh.

There was a ballroom on the lower level that would be the scene of the opening reception, Mr. Delacamp's Tuesday Tea, and all future luncheon meetings of the Boosters Club.

The guest rooms, furnished in Stickley, were Fran's chief pride. She said, "I've traveled extensively and stayed in luxury hotels with lavish furnishings but *no place to put anything down!* That's my pet peeve, and I designed these rooms to be functional as well as attractive."

Qwilleran asked, "Where will Mr. Delacamp camp while he's here?"

"In the presidential suite. No president ever stayed here, but there's still an adjoining room for the Secret Service, and it'll be used for his assistant."

"I hope he likes cats." Qwilleran pointed to a building across the street. An upstairs apartment had five windows with a cat in each, sitting on the sill and watching the flow of traffic below.

"Aren't they adorable?" Fran said. "They're watching pigeons on the roof of the inn."

"Or making a traffic survey. Who lives there?"

"Mrs. Sprenkle. The Sprenkle family owns the whole block. When her husband died, she sold their country house and moved downtown. She likes the action. He liked peace and quiet. Why does a man who can't stand noise marry a woman who can't stand silence?"

"It's the Jack Sprat law. She has unusual curtains. Is she a client of yours?"

"No. Amanda has done her work for forty years. It's all

Victorian. You'd hate it, Qwill! . . . And now, would you like to meet the manager before you leave? He's from Chicago."

The door to the manager's office on the second floor was standing open, and a clean-cut young man in suit and tie was working at the desk.

Fran said, "Barry, would you like to meet Mr. Q?"

Before she could make the introductions, he jumped up with hand extended. "I'm Barry Morghan, spelled with a GH."

"I'm Jim Qwilleran, spelled with a QW. Welcome to —"

"Excuse me, you guys. I have to run along," Fran said. "See you both at the reception."

"Have a chair, Mr. Qwilleran," said the manager.

"Call me Qwill. It's shorter, more forceful, and saves energy. I hear you're from Chicago. So am I, a Cubs fan from birth. What brings you to the backwoods?"

"Well, you see, I'd been assistant manager in a big hotel and decided this was a good career move. I'd always liked the hospitality field. My dad was a traveling man and sometimes took me along. I liked staying in different hotels, and my first ambition was to be a bellhop and wear one of those neat uniforms. I was pretty young then. Now I like the idea of being an innkeeper. I trained at Cornell."

"Would you say the inn is getting off to a good start?"

"Absolutely!" Barry consulted a calendar. "Champagne reception tomorrow night. Big family reunion on Labor Day. Formal afternoon tea Tuesday. Boosters Club luncheon Wednesday. All rooms booked for the Labor Day weekend and the Scottish weekend! And dinner reservations are going fast for the Mackintosh Room. We have this great chef from Chicago, you know. Your paper has interviewed him for Thursday's food page. The whole staff is excited. All the hiring was done before I got here—by Mr. Barter's office. It was his idea to hire MCCC students part-time. He's a great guy!"

G. Allen Barter was junior partner in the Pickax law firm of Hasselrich Bennett & Barter, and he was Qwilleran's representative in all matters pertaining to the Klingenschoen Foundation. Since the K Fund owned the inn, he was CEO.

Qwilleran said, "I know Bart very well. He says you need a place to live, and there's a carriage house apartment on my property that's available—four rooms, furnished. It's only a few blocks from downtown."

"Great! I'll take it!" the manager said. "I've been sleeping here, but I've got a van full of personal belongings that I'd like to offload."

"You'd better look at it first," Qwilleran said. "I'll show it to you any time."

"How about right now?"

Within minutes he was following Qwilleran's vehicle south on Main Street, around the Park Circle and into the parking lot of the K Theatre. They stopped at a fieldstone carriage house with carriage lanterns on all four corners.

"Great!" he exclaimed as he jumped out of his van.

"I warn you, the stairs are narrow and steep. It was built in the nineteenth century when people had small feet and narrow shoulders. You'll be interested to know it's said to be haunted—by a young woman whose name was Daisy."

"Great!"

"After you unpack, you can drive through the woods to my place, and I'll offer you a drink."

"Great!"

"By the way," Qwilleran said, "how do you feel about cats?"

"Anything that walks on four legs and doesn't bite is a friend of mine!"

By the time Barry Morghan arrived at the barn, the Siamese had been fed and were curled up like shrimp on their respective bar stools, sound asleep. Qwilleran went to the barnyard to greet him. He enjoyed newcomers' expressions of disbelief and awe when the hundred-year-old barn loomed before their eyes and he was not disappointed by his tenant's reaction. "Great!" he said with fervor.

The interior with its ramps and balconies and giant white cube sent him into further exclamations of astonishment.

"What do you like to drink? I have a well-stocked bar," Qwilleran said.

"I'm not much of a drinker. What are you going to have?"

"Ginger ale."

"Great! I'll have the same." Barry had changed into casualwear and walked around with his hands in his pants pockets, making comments. "Are those your cats, or are they fur cushions on the bar stools? . . . Have you read all those books? . . . I see you have one of those 'bent' bikes. Do you ride it?"

There was a recumbent bicycle leaning against a stone wall near the foyer. "It was a gift," Qwilleran explained. "Now that I'm used to pedaling with my feet elevated, I like it."

They lounged in the library area with their ginger ale, and his guest said, "Mind if I chew gum? I'm trying to stop smoking."

"Go right ahead."

"Is this a wastebasket?" He dropped the wrapper in a polished wooden receptacle with a carved top-handle.

"It's a wastebasket moonlighting as an antique Chinese water bucket, or vice versa. . . . Do you know I haven't chewed gum since I gave up baseball? It was part of the game for me: chomp gum, jerk cap, punch glove, hitch belt."

"Why did you give up baseball?"

"I came out of the military with a bum knee. It plagued me till I moved to Moose County and then disappeared. The natives credited the drinking water. I think the biking cured it."

Then the talk turned to the inn: how it had been dreary but clean, how everyone hated the food, how Fran Brodie had worked wonders with the interior. "She's one of our civic treasures," Qwilleran said.

"Yeah, she's a dynamo! Is she married?"

"No, but they're standing in line. Take a number."

"What's a good way to meet girls around here?" Barry asked. "Interesting ones, I mean."

"It depends on your definition of interesting. There

are numerous clubs you can join: theatre, bridge, golf, bird-watching, biking, hiking, and so forth. You can take a class at the art center, go to church, attend Boosters Club luncheons and meet spirited young businesswomen. How about volunteering to teach adults how to read and write? It would look good on your résumé," Qwilleran concluded. "Or in your obituary."

"Yow!" came an aggressive comment from a bar stool, where Koko was stretching and yawning.

"That's Kao K'o Kung, the brains of the family," Qwilleran said. "He reads minds, knows when the phone is going to ring, and tells time without looking at a clock—all skills denied to you and me. . . . Yum Yum is our glamorcat. She walks like a model on a runway, strikes photogenic poses, and melts hearts with her innocent gaze. But don't be fooled. She'll steal anything small and shiny."

The newcomer, dubious about Qwilleran's seriousness, changed the subject. "This is my first experience in a small town. Do you have any advice for me? I mean it! I want to get off on the right foot."

"The main thing," Qwilleran began, "is to remember that everyone knows everyone. Never speak ill of someone; you may be talking to his cousin or son-in-law or fellow clubmember. Play it safe by keeping your eyes and ears open and your mouth closed."

"Great . . . And one more question. My older brother likes winter sports and wouldn't mind moving up here. He's a doctor. He'd open a clinic."

"What kind of doctor?"

"Well, that's a family joke. My mother was an RN in

obstetrics, and she wanted my brother to be an OB, but he chose to go into dermatology because his patients don't call him up in the middle of the night."

Qwilleran chuckled. "All kidding aside, we need your brother. The nearest dermatologist is in the next county."

"Great! . . . He considers a small town a good place to raise a family—away from the muggings, car thefts, and shootings that make city life hairy."

"Yow!" came a loud comment in a minor key.

three

SATURDAY, SEPTEMBER 5—*Birds of a feather flock together.*

For the first time the daily adage on Culvert's calendar was accidentally apt. In the evening all the prominent birds of Moose County would wear their finest feathers to a charity reception benefiting the cause of literacy. They would be the first to inspect the new Mackintosh Inn and would see their names in the *Moose County Something* on Monday—perhaps even their photos.

For this special occasion Qwilleran dressed in Highland evening attire: a kilt in the Mackintosh tartan, a silver-mounted fur sporran, and a dagger in the cuff of his kilt-hose—this with the usual dinner jacket and black tie. Polly wore her white dinner dress with opal jewelry and a shoulder-sash in the Robertson tartan. If asked, she would be pleased to explain that (a) she was a Duncan by marriage and (b) the chief of the Robertson clan had been Duncan of Atholia, a descendent of Celtic earls and kinsman of Robert the Bruce. It amused her to tell them more than they really wanted to know.

They drove to the reception in her sedan, which seemed more compatible with a white dress and opals— more suitable than a big brown van. She said, "The mayor will be there. How do you think he'll react to Amanda's challenge?"

"He's a cool cucumber. He won't let on he knows his goose is cooked."

At the carriage entrance of the inn they were met by a valet crew of MCCC students who parked their car, leaving them to walk across a red carpet between a battery of media cameras.

"Just like a Hollywood premiere," Qwilleran remarked.

"Not exactly," she said, glancing at the vintage finery worn by the older guests. These last remaining descendants of the old moneyed families might be aged and infirm but they always turned out in evening attire to support a good cause. The Old Guard, they were affectionately called. Local wags called them the Mothball Brigade; a faint aroma of PCB hovered around the paisley shawls, sable stoles and outdated dinner jackets that came out of deep storage for the occasion.

The carriage entrance opened into a ground-level lobby with a grand staircase: half a flight up to the main lobby, half a flight down to the ballroom where the champagne was flowing. Like everyone else, Qwilleran and Polly took the descending flight, stopping partway to survey the subterranean hall. It was a scene of glowing chandeliers, huge bouquets of flowers, and hors d'oeuvre tables lighted by candles. Guests stood in clusters, holding champagne glasses. A string trio was playing Viennese waltzes. Servers circulated with trays of champagne and white grape juice.

There were hot and cold hors d'oeuvre tables, and Arch and Mildred Riker were standing at the former, critiquing the bite-size morsels. She was food editor of the *Something*; her husband was publisher of the paper. Both had the appearance of being happily well-fed.

Qwilleran said to Arch, "I knew I'd find you feeding at the trough." They were lifelong friends with a license to banter.

"Don't worry. I've left a few scraps for you."

Mildred said, "Try these delightful little crabmeat nothings! I must ask the chef his secret."

"He won't tell you," her husband said.

"Oh, yes, he will! I interviewed him yesterday, and we turned out to be soulmates. Read all about it on Thursday's food page, dear."

Qwilleran said, "How would you two like to be our guests in the Mackintosh Room next Saturday night? I'll reserve a table."

"They're booked solid," Arch said. "You're too late."

"Want to bet? The manager and I are soulmates." He spoke confidently, having made the reservation the day before.

He and Arch had been bickering chums since boyhood, and sparring was an ongoing way of expressing their friendship.

"Listen!" Mildred said, "They're playing *The Skater's Waltz*. It always makes me feel young and thin."

"Nothing ever makes me feel young and thin," Arch complained.

Eventually the foursome drifted away from the crabmeat soufflés, quiche tartlets, smoked trout canapés and goat cheese puffs. They mingled with the other guests:

Mayor Blythe, being overly charming.

Amanda Goodwinter, looking dowdy in her thirty-year-old dinner dress. She scowled at the admirers who clustered about her.

Whannell MacWhannell, the tax consultant, a big Scot wearing a kilt.

Don Exbridge, the developer, wearing a plaid cummerbund that was all wrong, Big Mac and Qwilleran agreed.

Fran Brodie, glamorous in a silvery sheath slit to mid-thigh.

Dr. Prelligate, president of MCCC, being overly attentive to Fran.

Carol and Larry Lanspeak, modestly inconspicuous as usual, although they were leading lights in the community.

Polly introduced Qwilleran to members of her library board, and he introduced the innkeeper to Polly.

The young man said, "Lucky I brought my tux! I didn't think I'd need it 400 miles north of everywhere, but my mother said I might want to get married."

Polly whispered to Qwilleran, "He won't have long to wait. He has good looks and personality."

"And a good job," Qwilleran mumbled.

Suddenly the music stopped, the lights blinked for attention, and a bagpiper swaggered into the hall playing *Scotland the Brave.* He was Andrew Brodie, the police chief, doing what he liked best.

Then the mayor stepped to the microphone and thanked the Klingenschoen Foundation for revitalizing downtown's foremost landmark. G. Allen Barter thanked Fran Brodie for her creative input. She thanked the K Fund for supplying the wherewithal so generously. And Barry Morghan thanked his lucky stars for bringing him to Pickax as innkeeper. "You're invited to tour the facility from bottom to top," he told the guests, "and continue to enjoy our hospitality here and in Rennie's coffee shop." There was a stampede up the stairs to the main lobby.

When Polly saw the portrait, she cried, "Qwill! She's lovely! So serene! So distinguished! I'm going to call her Lady Anne, after the heroine of the Scottish Rebellion. I must congratulate Paul Skumble!"

The artist, looking like a gnome in his bifurcated beard, was talking to prospective patrons. He had painted Polly's portrait earlier in the year, and when he saw her he opened his arms wide and said, "Baby, you look like an angel!"

She responded with light laughter, while Qwilleran said to the artist, "And you look like the devil."

"I feel like a penguin in these duds."

"You don't look like one. They have shorter legs."

Polly interrupted the banter. "Paul, you're a genius. You painted Lady Anne's soul!"

"That's my specialty. Painting souls."

The police chief was wandering around the lobby looking dumbfounded at the decor. "Pretty fancy," he said to Qwilleran.

"Your daughter deserves credit for doing a great job! The old hotel was grim."

"But it was clean," Brodie said.

"Will your department be busy next week, guarding the jewels?"

"Nah. He doesn't need anything from us. He's been here lots of times without incident. It's all private. Valuables kept in the hotel safe. No problem."

Someone clutched Qwilleran's arm and said, "That portrait spooks me!" It was Arch Riker. "It's exactly how she looked when we were growing up. I'd go over to your house, and she'd play *Flight of the Bumblebee* for me. I always listened with my mouth hanging open; how could fingers move so fast?"

"Yes, she was good at vivace, wasn't she?"

"All you could play was *Humoresque*, double slow."

"I was faster at stealing second base," Qwilleran said ruefully. "I sometimes wish I'd practiced more, but the piano was not my forte."

At that moment the publicity man interrupted. He wanted a shot of Qwilleran with the painting.

"Only if the artist is included," he replied. "I'm here as an accident of birth; Skumble deserves the credit for doing the impossible."

In a lobby alcove outfitted as a reading room Fran Brodie was giving a tour-guide spiel on Gustav Stickley. A portrait of the turn-of-the-century cabinet-maker hung on the wall; he wore a bow tie, pince-nez glasses on a cord, and a cryptic smile.

"What did that smile mean?" Fran asked her small audience, all of whom seemed enraptured by her melodious voice and stunning gown. "He was a writer, philosopher, and cabinetmaker, and yet he came from humble beginnings on a Wisconsin farm, the eldest of eleven children. Cruel fate made him head of the family at the age of twelve, and he had to drop out of school and work in a stoneyard. Still, he educated himself by reading. He hated stone and developed a passion for wood. His furniture designs with plain, honest structural lines and a reverence for wood were made from 1901 to 1915 and had many imitators. . . . The framed pictures grouped over the trestle tables are enlargements of the 'cozy cottage' drawings in Stickley's magazine, *The Craftsman*."

Another center of attention in the lobby was the new reception desk with its front panel of iridescent ceramic tiles typical of the period. Behind it stood four young persons in black blazers with the Mackintosh crest. One of them was Lenny Inchpot, who had been on the desk when the bomb went off and a chandelier fell in the lobby. He still had a slight scar on his forehead. Now he was captain of the desk clerks, who worked in four six-hour shifts. He himself worked evenings. All were MCCC students.

Viyella, a vibrant young woman who worked afternoons, said, "I love meeting people! This is an exciting place to work."

Marietta, on mornings, was intensely serious. She hoped to learn a lot on the job.

Boze, on duty midnight to six, was a big fellow with bland smile. "Hi!" he mumbled.

Larry said, "Boze will be tossing the caber at the Highland Games. We're all rooting for him."

"I'll be there," Qwilleran promised.

Polly drew him aside. "I want you to meet the liveliest, most sensible woman on my library board: Magdalene Sprenkle. She's wearing the famous Sprenkle torsade tonight."

"Should I know what that is?"

"A necklace of twisted strands. Hers is diamonds and pearls. She's hoping to sell it to Mr. Delacamp this year. When her husband was alive, he wouldn't let her part with something that had been in the family for generations."

The woman in black velvet and a dazzling choker had a majestic build and hearty manner, and there were cat hairs on the front of her dress. "Call me Maggie," she said, "because I'm going to call you Qwill."

"Do you happen to have five cats?"

"I do, and I'd have more if I had more windows facing the afternoon sun. They're all strays, adopted from the animal shelter, and they're all ladies!"

"Do I detect gender bias?"

"You do, sir! The ladies are sweeter and cuddlier, and yet they stand up for their rights."

He nodded as if in agreement. Actually he was thinking about Yum Yum with her sweet, ingratiating ways—and her shrieks of indignation if she didn't get what she wanted *when she wanted it!* "What are their names?" he asked, knowing that cat-fanciers liked to be asked.

"They're all named after famous women in history: Sarah, Charlotte, Carrie, Flora, and Louisa May."

"Hmmm," he murmured, recognizing a challenge. "Name them again—slowly."

"Sarah."

"Bernhardt?"

"Charlotte."

"Brontë, of course."

"Carrie."

"It's got to be Nation."

"Flora."

"I hope it's Macdonald."

"And Louisa May."

"That's the easiest. Alcott."

"You clever man! I'm going to give you a big hug!" She did, and several cat hairs were transferred from her black velvet to his dinner jacket. "You must come and meet my ladies-in-waiting. But no publicity, please."

Polly said, "But how about telling him your great-grandmother's story, Maggie? He's collecting legends of Moose County for a book. Its title will be *Short and Tall Tales*."

"When?" Maggie asked with her usual decisiveness.

"Friday?" He was never one to waste words.

The date was made. "Now I have to go and say hello to the mayor and give him a big hug," she said. "I'm a political hypocrite."

Qwilleran and Polly watched her cross the lobby and deposit some cat hairs on His Honor's dinner jacket.

Although the Mackintosh Room would not be serving until Tuesday evening, it was brightly lighted to show off the clan tartan on the chair seats and the Mackintosh crest on the wall. Derek Cuttlebrink, the six-foot-four busboy who had become a six-foot-eight maître d', was standing at the host's lectern, taking future reservations.

"Hi, Mr. Q! I see you've booked a table for next Saturday," he said.

"I hope the lights are on a rheostat."

"Oh sure. We'll turn them way down when we serve. Have you seen the coffee shop? It's kind of far-out for Pickax."

Fran Brodie was now standing at the entrance to Rennie's, the converted coffee shop, answering questions. "This was inspired by a Charles Rennie Mackintosh tearoom in Glasgow, designed in the early twentieth century. . . . Yes, it will be on network TV, but I don't know exactly when. . . . Two magazines have already photographed it. . . . Well, I see Rennie's as a stimulating place for an overnight guest to have breakfast, an exciting place for out-of-towners to have lunch or dinner, and a friendly place to have a snack after a tap-dance class. . . . Yes, you can go in and take a table. They're serving refreshments."

A framed photograph of the Scottish architect with flowing moustache and an artist's flowing silk tie was hanging in the entrance.

Fran said to Qwilleran, "Ancestor of yours? You have his moustache and his eyes."

The distinguishing feature of Rennie's was the high-backed Mackintosh chair, about four feet tall and tapered upward. Lacquered black, these chairs surrounded tables lacquered in bright blue or bright green. The white walls were decorated with black line drawings of oversize flowers. Napkins were a bold black-and-white stripe.

Carol and Larry Lanspeak, seated at a blue table, waved an invitation to Qwilleran and Polly to join them. Everyone liked the Lanspeaks, the affluent but down-to-earth owners of the department store. Both had given up acting careers in New York to carry on the family retailing tradition. Their talents were still put to good use in the theatre club, and all other community projects received their generous support.

Tonight they were in a festive mood and Larry raised his champagne glass in a toast to the Mackintosh Inn.

"Here's to the K Fund!" said Carol.

"Here's to Aunt Fanny Klingenschoen!" Qwilleran said.

"Here's to Lady Anne," Polly murmured.

Carol asked her about her vacation.

"My sister and I went to Toronto, Montreal, and Quebec City and met the most charming French-Canadian professor. He wants to come here to study Canadian influence in our pioneer days."

Qwilleran said, "I spent my vacation in Mooseville and Fishport."

"Ah! Fishport!" Larry declaimed in his stage voice. "The home of the covered dish! Where the Hawleys speak only to Scottens, and the Scottens speak only to fish!"

"I didn't see any covered dishes in Fishport. Should I know what a covered dish is?" Qwilleran asked innocently.

"Why, it's a dish to pass at a potluck supper!" Carol informed him. "Don't you go to potluck suppers?"

"Not if I can help it."

"Once a city boy, always a city boy," Polly explained.

"How does Delacamp feel about potluck suppers?"

Larry said, "He's a consummate snob."

"Let me describe his program," Carol offered. "He and his assistant arrive on Labor Day by chartered plane. Larry and I greet him at the airport and turn over the Mercedes rental car that he has requested. That evening he's guest of honor at a dinner at the country club. Tuesday afternoon he gives a tea for prospective customers. Guests view his private collection of jewelry and make appointments to go to his suite and buy. Those who have heirloom jewelry to sell make appointments for him to visit their homes."

Polly said, "I hear Don Exbridge is furious because his second wife isn't even invited to the tea, while his first wife is invited to pour."

Qwilleran said, "I'd like to see what goes on at this affair. Would my press card get me in? I wouldn't write about it—just look."

"No no no!" Carol said. "It's for women only. Even Larry isn't admitted, and he sponsors the whole thing."

Her husband said, "Old Campo thinks women are more impressionable when their husbands aren't around. They're more likely to spend money."

Qwilleran listened in amazement. He was not about to give up. "Perhaps you could sneak me in as part of the wait staff."

"The servers are all young women dressed as French maids, Qwill."

"If it weren't for my moustache, I could go in drag."

Laughter erupted around the blue table.

"Why are you so determined to crash the party?" Carol asked.

"I'm congenitally nosy, and I have a professional curiosity."

Polly said, "Hell hath no fury like a journalist denied access."

"You say the jewels are on display at the tea. What do they do about security?"

"Nothing. No one has any fears about a robbery, if that's what you're thinking."

"And no one had any fears about bombing last year. Times are changing. . . . No doubt Delacamp has the stuff insured, but in the case of a theft, would the inn be liable? Would Delacamp's insurance company sue the inn's insurance company? I think I should go as a security guard, so that the inn is covered."

There was a ripple of laughter around the table.

"I'm serious!"

Then Larry said with a grin, "Why not?" He himself had played practical jokes, masquerading as a stony-faced butler to enliven a stuffy dinner party . . . playing the role of a drunken citizen to stir up a dreary city council meeting.

"Yes. Why not?" Carol echoed.

They looked at each other with conspiratorial merriment.

"We could find him a uniform in the costume department."

"The cap should be a couple of sizes too large."

"Dark glasses."

"His moustache and hair should be darkened."

"He'd need a sidearm in a holster."

"There's a wooden gun in the prop room."

"How about a German shepherd?"

Suddenly the image of the county's richest citizen in a guard's uniform with dark glasses and a wooden gun struck them all as hilariously comic.

Then Polly, with her usual common sense, asked, "How will you explain this caper to Mr. Delacamp?"

Qwilleran was skilled at fabricating fiction on the spur of the moment. "Well . . . it's a new inn, with new owners, a new insurance policy. The terms require the inn to have a security guard on the premises when valuables are on exhibit."

"Sounds good to me," Larry said.

"I'll explain it to Barter," Qwilleran said. "He'll go along. He has a sense of humor."

four

Sunday, September 6—*Without a shepherd, sheep are not a flock.*

It was the second day of the craft fair. In the afternoon Qwilleran and Polly walked down the lane to the art center. She had a long list and expected to do most of her Christmas shopping. It was Qwilleran's custom to give edibles and potables for the holidays, but he hoped to find a good-looking pencil-holder for the library table. They saw hand-thrown pots, hand-woven placemats, hand-painted tiles, hand-wrought iron rivets, hand-screened scarves, hand-carved wood salad servers, hand-printed notecards, and hand-stitched wall hangings.

Then Qwilleran saw Thornton's woodturnings: bowls, plates, candlesticks, vases, and such—lathed to a satin smoothness and decorated with nature's own markings. There were captivating streaks, swirls, wisps, splotches, and squiggles in tints of brown on the pale waxed wood.

"I use spalted wood," Thornton explained. "Irregularities caused by fungus, worms, faulty growth, or wood-peckers produce these abstract patterns when turned on a lathe."

Qwilleran pointed to a foot-tall container of classical shape with a marbleized veining. "I like that! Do you call it a vase, urn, jar, or what?"

"A vessel. The shape was used in ancient Egyptian times for transporting water or olive oil. It's turned from a chunk of spalted elm. The small round bowl with a lid is spalted maple."

"I'll take both of them."

"The small one's sold." There was a red sticker on the bottom of it with the initials M.R.

Qwilleran huffed into his moustache in frustration, then said, "How do you produce one of these . . . vessels?"

"First find a good burl."

"Should I know what that is?"

"It's an unnatural growth on a tree. You rough out your design, wax it, dry it for a few months, chuck it into place on your lathe, turn it, shape it with gouging tools, sand it, finish it with wax or oil."

"It obviously takes skill."

"And patience. And some intelligence, if you'll pardon my lack of modesty. You learn a lot about trees."

"Where did you learn how to do this craft?" Qwilleran asked.

"I took lessons from a master woodturner in Lockmaster, one-on-one. Believe me, I regret I'm getting such a late start. Woodturning could be a lifetime study."

To transport Polly's numerous purchases—and his own

spalted elm vessel—back to the barn, Qwilleran ran back up the lane and fetched his van.

"Where are you going to put the . . . vessel?" she asked.

"In the center of the coffee table." It was a low contemporary table, large and square, surrounded by upholstered seating.

"I think it's an absolutely stunning piece," she said when she saw it.

"You should have seen the one that got away," Qwilleran said. "It was smaller but spectacular—about the size of a grapefruit—a bowl with a domed cover and a small knob on top, turned-in-one with the cover. Amazing! But it was already sold."

He had forgotten to look for a pencil-holder. His fat yellow pencils were stuck in a brown coffee mug inscribed *As he brews, so shall he drink.* He offered anyone a dollar who could identify the author. So far, only Polly had collected.

LABOR DAY, SEPTEMBER 7—*When the cat's away, the mice will play.*

Qwilleran and Polly celebrated by driving out of town for a backyard barbecue. G. Allen Barter and his wife were hosting the party. They had invited the new innkeeper from Chicago and some young men and women of his own age, mostly paralegals from the office of Hasselrich Bennett & Barter.

The route from Pickax passed several abandoned mines from Moose County's distant past: the Big B mine, the Buckshot (scene of a recent cave-in), and the Old Glory.

The sites were fenced with chainlink and posted as dangerous, and each had a weathered wood shafthouse towering above the barren scene. These ghostly monuments had a haunting fascination for locals and visitors alike.

The Barter house was surrounded by working farms, and cocktails were served on a terrace with a view of a neighbor's grazing sheep, while chickens turned on a spit and corn roasted in the coals.

Someone asked the new innkeeper the inevitable question: "How do you like it up here?"

"Will someone please explain something?" he inquired. "What are those old wooden towers out in the middle of nowhere?"

The other young people looked at their boss, and Barter replied, "They're the shafthouses of mines that were highly productive in the nineteenth century but failed in the early twentieth. There are ten of them in the county."

"They should tear them down and fill in the mineshafts," said the brash newcomer from Down Below. "Then they could graze more sheep."

"Smile when you say that, chum," Qwilleran advised. "Those shafthouses are near and dear to the hearts of local folks. And tourists, too. In the souvenir shops the best-selling postcards have views of shafthouses. And there's a fine artist here who paints watercolors of shafthouses and can't turn them out fast enough to fill the demand."

"Somebody should write a book about all this!" said Barry.

"Somebody has!" several of the guests said in unison.

"It's in the library, if you're interested," Polly told him. Then she amused everyone by describing the Computer War, in which library subscribers picketed the building and burned their library cards on the front steps—all in protest against automation.

Qwilleran said, "The people here, you have to understand, Barry, are descended from pioneers, who were rugged individualists."

Everyone seemed to have a good time—not a boisterous good time but a civilized good time. When it was over, Qwilleran told Barter about the security guard stunt. The attorney laughed and called it a harmless joke. Then they confided in Barry, whose said, "Great!"

TUESDAY, SEPTEMBER 8—*Better a living dog than a dead lion.*

In the early afternoon Qwilleran left the barn for guard duty, saying goodbye to the sleeping cats on the bar stools and adding, "Wish me well, and I'll bring you a cucumber sandwich." Two pairs of ears twitched.

Carol Lanspeak and the wardrobe mistress were waiting for him at the K Theatre. The building was a giant cube of fieldstone, once upon a time the most magnificent residence in town. There the Klingenschoen family had lived in private splendor, spurned by the mining and lumbering magnates. Ironically, it was the K fortune that had recently doubled and trebled the quality of life in Moose County. As for the venerable building itself, it had barely survived disaster and now served as a theatre seating two hundred.

When Qwilleran arrived, Carol ushered him into the

backstage area, saying, "Isn't this a lark? With a little dye, dark glasses, and a visored cap, you'll never be recognized."

The Lanspeaks amazed Qwilleran. Nothing in their appearance or manners suggested that they had been on the stage, yet Carol could play a queen or a harlot convincingly, and Larry could play the role of scoundrel, old man, or dashing hero. Both had the inner energy that distinguished an outstanding performer.

Now Carol was saying, "It's the kind of dye that will wash right out when you get home, so you don't have to worry about that. The cats won't recognize you, though."

"Koko will, but Yum Yum will hiss at me."

"You trimmed your moustache a little. That's good."

"I always trim it for weddings and undercover assignments," he said.

"First choose your uniform. Then Alice can make alterations if necessary while I work on makeup." Alice Toddwhistle was standing by with a tape measure around her neck and a thimble on her finger.

Qwilleran chose a dark blue outfit with an emblem on the sleeve and a cap that looked official if not examined too closely. When he tried it on and appeared in the fitting room, the two women screamed at the sight: the trousers too short, the sleeves too long, the cap three sizes too large.

"Do you have a Neanderthal in the club?" he asked.

Alice said, "I can fix the pantlegs and sleeves in a jiffy. The cap will be okay if we stuff the crown with tissue paper."

In the makeup room Carol went to work with profes-

sional assurance, darkening the pepper-and-salt moustache, eyebrows, and patches of gray at his temples.

"Did Delacamp arrive on schedule?" he asked.

"Yes. He brought his niece this time—a quiet girl. She
defers to him all the time. He's put on some weight, but
he's quite handsome for a man of his age. I think he's had
cosmetic surgery. And his toupée is new. A very expensive one . . . Oops! Did I bump you in the eyeball? I'm
sorry."

"That's all right. I have another one."

"At the country club dinner he showed his slides of
fabulous jewels in museums. There was a necklace that
Napoleon gave Josephine, and it must have weighed a
pound: all rubies, emeralds, enamel work, and precious
metals. . . . Do you realize that rubies and emeralds were
replaced by diamonds in nineteenth-century fashion
for the simple reason that the lighting in public places
was improving! Dazzle became more important than
color. . . . There!" Carol whipped off the cape covering
his shoulders. "Now for the logistics: I'll drive you to the
inn. Barry Morghan will meet you at the entrance and
whisk you upstairs on the elevator. At three o'clock he'll
escort you to the ballroom. As soon as it's over, return to
his office. He'll phone the store, and Larry will drive you
back here."

Qwilleran said, "Carol, you're so well organized, it's
unnerving."

"Well, it helps if you've run a department store for
twenty-five years . . . and directed two dozen stage productions . . . and raised three kids."

As Qwilleran knew, their elder son was a clergyman in

New York State; their daughter was an M.D. in Pickax; the younger son had been a tragic failure. No one ever mentioned him. "How does Dr. Diane feel about pouring tea this afternoon?" Qwilleran asked.

"She says she hasn't been so nervous since she lanced her first boil! She and Polly will pour for forty-five minutes and then be relieved by Susan Exbridge and Maggie Spenkle. It's Maggie's Belgian lace banquet cloth that we're using, and Susan is lending two silver tea services and a six-branch silver candelabrum."

Then the uniform was ready. Qwilleran assembled his disguise and looked in the mirror.

"Well?" Carol asked.

"Well?" Alice repeated.

He hesitated. "I don't know who this guy is, but he's not me!"

The women applauded.

As Carol drove him to the inn, Qwilleran asked, "Do you know a perfume called L'Heure Bleue?"

"Of course! It's a classic. A delicate flowery fragrance with a hint of vanilla. Jacque Guerlain created it for Yvonne Printemps in 1912. As a matter of fact, Larry gave me a bottle of L'Heure Bleue when we were honeymooning in Paris umpteen years ago."

"Could you special-order it? I'd like to surprise Polly."

"Be glad to. I think she'd like the eau de toilette in the spray bottle. . . . And by the way, are you and she free on Thursday evening? We're giving a small at-home dinner for Mr. Delacamp and his niece. For you, Qwill, it would be your only opportunity to meet him. . . . But I warn you, he's a non-stop talker."

"That's okay, as long as I learn something."

"You will, believe me! He's an encyclopedia of facts about several subjects."

They could see Barry Morghan standing at the carriage entrance of the inn.

"Okay," said Qwilleran. "I've taken my adjustment. I'm Joe Buzzard, ex-cop. I hire out for security gigs. Everyone's a potential jewel thief."

He stomped out of the Lanspeak van and swaggered up to the entrance in a surly manner, pretending not to see Barry.

With a straight face the innkeeper asked, "Are you from City Security Services?"

"Yes, sir."

"Follow me."

As soon as they were in the office with the door closed, Barry said, "You look great, Qwill! No one will recognize you. How about some coffee while we're waiting for three o'clock? Can you drink without the dye running down your chin?"

"I'd feel safer with a straw. . . . How did you enjoy the barbecue?"

"I had a great time! Lots of nice people. They're not uptight like city dudes."

"They're friendly, no doubt about it, but they're also nosy and prone to spread rumors, so be on your guard."

"Speaking of city types," Barry said, "guess who barged into my office this morning—wearing a Moroccan caftan and five pounds of silver jewelry! He said coolly, 'I'm

Delacamp.' I jumped up to welcome him and got the tips of his fingers for a handshake. He had a complaint to make. He had gone to the kitchen to tell them how he wanted the tea made, and the chef—he said—was unco-operative and rude. I apologized for him but pointed out that Board of Health regulations put the kitchen off lim-its to anyone not involved officially in food service."

"I'd say you handled that well, Barry."

"I thought so, too. . . . Wait a minute, Qwill. You need something else. An intercom! I'll get you one. Hang it on your belt."

The focal point of the ballroom was a long tea table with lace cloth, tall silver candelabrum, and two flower arrangements. At each end a silver tea service stood ready. Small skirted tables and clusters of little ballroom chairs were scattered about the room. There was a piano in one corner, half hidden by large potted plants. And off to one side was the jewel table, covered with an Oriental rug. There were no jewels in sight—just leather carrying cases. A hatted young woman in a businesslike suit was in charge.

At Barry's suggestion Qwilleran stationed himself on the stairs in a shadowy corner from which he could ob-serve without being conspicuous. When Polly and Dr. Diane arrived, they brushed past him without noticing and went to opposite ends of the tea table—Polly in a simple blue Breton to match her dress, Diane in a toque with an impudently long pheasant feather. Then the servers brought platters of finger food and silver pots of tea to place on the burners. It would take more than a

an older woman who worked as office manager at the *Moose County Something*. She lived quietly, and her hobby was button collecting. Surely she was not in the market for a diamond clip. Did she have family heirlooms to sell? Her ancestors had been either shipbuilders or bootleggers, depending on the source of gossip.

Who was there to buy and who was there to sell? As Qwilleran deduced, the potential buyers pored over the jewels in the shallow trays, then spoke to the assistant, who wrote something in a black leather notebook. The potential sellers, on the other hand, ignored the display and merely spoke to the assistant, who again wrote in the book.

What did Delacamp think of the outrageous hats? Did he realize the guests were mocking him? Polly's blue Breton was one of the few sane and simple hats in the hall. Qwilleran named it L'Heure Bleue. Others he named Swan Lake . . . Fruit Salad Plate . . . Yes We Have No Bananas . . . or Wreck of the Hesperus. It killed time.

At that point male footsteps came tripping down the stairs behind him and stopped just behind his right shoulder. A hushed voice asked, "How's everything?"

"Boring!" Qwilleran muttered without turning his head.

"Anything I can do?" the innkeeper asked.

"Yes. Turn on the sprinkling system."

"It's stuffy in here. I'll check the ventilators. . . . At four-thirty make your getaway and come to my office. Use the stairway."

Then Qwilleran was alone again. According to his watch, he had another half-hour to spend as Joe Buzzard of City Security Services. He tried rising on his toes, stretching his spine, flexing his muscles discreetly, blinking his eyes behind his dark glasses.

Polly had finished her duty at the tea table and was now circulating and chatting with other guests. She knew everyone! Gradually she made her way to the jewel table. He had told her to select something nice; it would be her Christmas present. She protested; she had her pearls and her opals, and she had no taste for diamonds. He had insisted, however, and now he saw her approach the leather cases reluctantly . . . explain to the assistant . . . look at shallow trays of baubles and shake her head . . . then show sudden interest, even enthusiasm. The assistant wrote something in her book, and Polly had another cup of tea.

Now what? Qwilleran consulted his watch. Twenty minutes more! He began to wish for a minor jewel heist, and he fantasized a scenario:

French maid drops a platter of cucumber sandwiches to divert attention . . . grabs an empty teapot and bashes jeweler's assistant . . . scoops handfuls of diamonds into her apron . . . dashes to the service exit pursued by a security guard waving a wooden gun and shouting "Stop thief!"

This exercise amused Qwilleran for five minutes.

Fifteen minutes more!

Now what?

He could search for fodder for the "Qwill Pen." Could he write a thousand words on cucumber sandwiches . . . or the forgotten art of hand-kissing . . . or hats? Yes! There were cowboy hats, baseball caps, bike helmets, construction workers' hardhats, a bagpiper's bonnet, gob hats, a bishop's miter. Hats were important! There had been George Washington's cocked hat, Yankee Doodle's hat with a feather, Humphrey Bogart's snap-brim fedora, Maurice Chevalier's straw boater, Fred Astaire's silk top hat . . .

Before Qwilleran knew it, the piano music stopped, the tea-warmers were turned off, the jewel cases were locked, and he was running up the stairs to the inn-keeper's office, gasping for a cup of coffee.

When Larry Lanspeak drove him back to the K Theatre, Qwilleran said, "Well, your jeweler camps it up, doesn't he? His get-up is straight out of Ara-bian Nights, and his manners date back to Molière. . . . And you'll have to forgive me, Larry, but I can't help wondering if this hoopla is worthwhile—businesswise, that is."

Larry said, "I'll be frank with you. We don't get a penny of commission from any of his transactions here, but—what the heck?—it's only once every five years, and in between, if a customer of ours wants to special-order a string of pearls or an engagement ring, we get the usual mark-up. Also, the ballyhoo is good public relations for us. It helps the Old Guard unload some of their old jew-elry."

"Do you think he offers them a fair price?"

"No one ever complains. He sends them roses, and they're always thrilled to have him visit their homes."

Larry dropped Qwilleran at the side door of the the-atre, handing him a small paperbound booklet. "Here's a script of the play that's about to open, in case you want to read it before opening night. . . . I assume you'll be reviewing it for the paper."

"Who else?" It was a script for *Night Must Fall.*

"It was first produced in 1937. Emlyn Williams wrote the role of the houseboy for himself. It's a challenge for an actor."

"Yes, I know," Qwilleran said. "I saw a revival on Broadway several years ago. I suppose Derek Cuttlebrink will be playing the Emlyn Williams role."

"Unfortunately, no. He could bring it off, but he's working nights at the inn. He's maître d' of the Mackintosh Room, you know. . . . Just leave your uniform and props on the table in the costume department, Qwill."

"Okay, and thanks for everything, Larry. It was . . . an unforgettable experience."

Qwilleran had misgivings about Derek as maître d'. The last two restaurants he managed had closed suddenly and permanently—one under a cloud of scandal, one under a cloud of dust.

In the late evening, when Qwilleran phoned Polly to report, Koko came running and hopped on the library table. Did he feel obliged to chaperon the conversation? Did he know there was a Siamese male named Brutus at the other end of the line? Or was he still trying to figure out how the mystifying instrument worked?

Her first words were, "Well, was the experience worth your while?"

"Not really," he said. "What did you think of the hats?"

"They were just teasing Mr. Delacamp. He pretended to think they were fabulous."

"What did you think of his private collection?"

"He had some spectacular things, such as a vintage pin paced with thirteen carats of diamonds—and signed. He was asking thirty-five thousand."

"It won't sell in Moose County!"

"Don't be too sure. Signed pieces are collectible, and there are persons of means around here who buy for investment but never advertise the fact. I saw a solid gold Tiffany tea-strainer for eighteen hundred that was already sold. It won't be used to strain tea!"

"Did you find something you like?"

"Yes, I did!" she said with enthusiasm. "A cameo ring!"

"A *cameo!*" His tone indicated a distaste for cameos.

"Not the commercial quality that's sold to tourists, Qwill. Antique cameos with incredibly fine carving are making a comeback. I saw a pin depicting Venus and Cupid in a forest, and the carving was so detailed, I could count the leaves on the trees! The ring, though, is something I can see myself wearing. The subject is the Three Graces in a gold mounting. They're the goddesses of beauty, refinement, and the arts."

"It sounds like you, Polly. Grab it!"

"They're holding it for me. My appointment is Thursday at two."

"Good! I'll write a check. How much?"

"They don't accept checks or credit cards—only cash."

"That's odd," he said, thinking of the diamond pin for thirty-five thousand. "But it's all right. I'll make a withdrawal Thursday morning and deliver it to you at the library—or even in the lobby of the inn at two o'clock. . . . How much?"

"Eight hundred."

"Is that all? I had visions of eighteen thousand! I was prepared to hire an armored truck from the bank."

"Actually," she said with a ripple of laughter, "it's only seven-ninety-five. And that includes tax."

"I'll withdraw eight hundred, and be sure to get your five dollars change."

Qwilleran replaced the receiver thoughtfully as he questioned the terms of sale: cash only . . . no tax.

"What do you think of that gambit?" he asked Koko, who was sitting near the phone.

The cat jumped to the floor and walked slowly and with deliberation to the kitchen cabinet where the Kabibbles were stored, while Yum Yum shrieked from the top of the refrigerator, hitting a high C that would curdle one's blood.

five

WEDNESDAY, SEPTEMBER 9—*Chickens always come home to roost.*

After the Siamese had breakfasted and performed their morning ablutions (three licks to the paw, four swipes over the ear, etc.), they were treated to a workout with Qwilleran's old paisley tie. He enjoyed whipping it around over their heads and watching their midair contortions. When they were tired and ready to stretch out in a patch of morning sun, he went to his studio on the first balcony to work on the "Qwill Pen" column for Friday.

Halfway through a sentence he was interrupted by urgent yowling on the main floor, and he took the shortcut to the kitchen, down the spiral staircase. Koko was standing on the kitchen counter, staring out the window. Qwilleran made a quick check. There were no vehicles in the barnyard, no prowlers on the grounds. "False alarm!" he said to the cat. "You can get arrested for that!"

Just then a small red car came bouncing through the

wooded area and pulled up to the kitchen door. Koko knew it was coming, certainly knew who was driving, and probably knew what she was bringing!

"My apologies, old boy," Qwilleran said. Going out to greet the visitor, he exclaimed, "Celia! What a pleasant surprise!"

"Look in the backseat, Chief. There's some stuff for your freezer. I was gonna sneak in and leave it in the pirate chest." A weathered sea chest stood at the back door for package deliveries.

"No one sneaks in when the Inspector General is on duty."

Celia laughed happily. She always laughed at the mildest quip from "the Chief." She explained, "I've brought you two meals of macaroni and cheese and a two-pound meatloaf. It's sliced so you can thaw some for a sandwich. I didn't put much onion in it because you might like to give some to the kitties, and I know they're particular. . . . Ooh! You have new bar stools!" she squealed when she went indoors. "We're so busy! I had to hire a helper. We're catering a wedding reception Saturday."

"Will you have time left for volunteer work? You were a real asset."

"Only one thing—teaching adults to read. My first student is a forty-year-old woman who's tickled to be able to read recipe books. In fact, she's the one I hired as my helper. . . . Have you rented my old apartment yet?"

"To the new manager of the Mackintosh Inn. He says he has a strange feeling that some wonderful person lived there before him."

"Oh, Chief! You're a big kidder!"

. . .

In mid-afternoon Qwilleran walked downtown to Lois's Luncheonette for a slice of her famous apple pie. Lois Inchpot was a loud, bossy, good-hearted woman who had been feeding downtown shoppers and workers for decades—in a dingy backstreet lunchroom. The shabbier it became with the years, the more the customers cherished it; they felt comfortable there.

When Qwilleran arrived, the place was empty, and Lois was in the kitchen, working on dinner. "Whaddaya want?" came a demanding voice through the pass-through window.

"Apple pie and a cuppa!" he shouted back.

"Apple's all gone! You can have cherry."

He walked to the pass-through and said, "I'm not enthusiastic about cherry pie."

"How come? You un-American—or something?"

"I did my patriotic bit when I helped choose the queen for the cherry festival."

Lois shoved a mug of coffee across the shelf and then banged a plate of cherry pie beside it, chanting, "Cherries every day keep the gout away!"

"Is that propaganda for the cherry-growers? Or are you practicing medicine without a license?"

"Eat it!" she ordered. "You'll love it!"

He had to admit the pie was good—not too tart, not too sweet, not too gelatinous, not too soupy. Obviously it had never been in a freezer or a microwave oven. "Not bad!" he declared as he returned his empty plate. "Keep practicing, and someday you'll get it right."

"Oh, pish posh!" she said grouchily but with a half smile. She liked Qwilleran.

"Where's Lenny?"

Her voice softened. "He has classes 'most all day on Wednesday, and I don't allow nothin' to interfere with that boy's education. He'll finish school if I hafta scrub floors! Did you know he's workin' part-time at the hotel?—I mean, the inn? Six to midnight. And he's captain of the desk clerks," she said proudly.

"Someday he'll be chief innkeeper," Qwilleran predicted, knowing that was what she wanted to hear.

"Lenny says old Mr. Muckety-Muck is here again, registered in the fancy suite on the third floor. You seen him?"

"To *whom* . . . are you referring?" Qwilleran asked to tease her.

"Don't get la-de-da with me! You know who I mean."

"No, I haven't seen him. I thought I might catch a glimpse of him here, eating cherry pie."

"Hah!" she huffed with contempt, banging the lid on a soup kettle for emphasis.

Just then her son burst into the restaurant and threw his textbooks on a table in the rear booth. "Got any pie, Mom?" He helped himself to a mug of coffee. "Hi, Mr. Q! Going to the games this weekend? The inn's booked solid for Friday and Saturday nights."

"Do you participate in the athletic events, Lenny?"

"Only the footraces. I leave the hammer-throw and all that to the big guys, but our night clerk tosses the caber. He has the strength for it. I introduced him to you at the party Saturday night. We call him Boze, short for Bozo."

Lenny moved his coffee mug to Qwilleran's table. "I'm sort of his manager. He needs somebody to prod him, make his decisions, keep him on track, you know."

"How long have you known him?"

"Since high school. I was managing the football team, and Boze was a great tackle. Not much of a student, though, and he wanted to drop out. So my mom and I took him on as a private crusade. I tutored him, and she fed him and read the riot act. She's good at both of those! . . . And he managed to squeak by with a diploma."

"What were his parents doing all this time?"

"He's an orphan. Grew up in different foster homes. After graduation he got a job as woodsman with a forestry company, and I worked at the old hotel until it was bombed."

"What brought Boze out of the woods?" Qwilleran asked.

"A soft job at the hotel, a small scholarship to MCCC, and a berth on the Moose County team for the Highland Games. Boze can toss the caber like nothing you ever saw! It's not just brute strength, you know. It's tricky, and he's mastered the knack."

"Should I know what a caber is?"

"It's a pole—a tree trunk—about twenty feet long and weighing about two hundred pounds. Boze tosses it like a toothpick and tumbles it end-over-end, the way you're supposed to. If we can beat those Bixby bums Saturday, it'll give the whole county a big charge. Are you gonna be there?"

"I've never attended a Scottish Gathering, but I'll be

there, rooting for you guys. Altogether it's quite a lively week in the sleepy town of Pickax. Have you met the distinguished guest?"

"No, he checked in while Viyella was on the desk. She says he comes on pretty strong, but his niece is kind of mousy. Not after eleven o'clock when I'm on the desk, though! I guess her uncle's gone to bed, and she comes down to the lobby in false eyelashes, short-short skirts and lots of lipstick. She likes to hang around the desk and talk about rock bands. I couldn't care less. I go for country-western. Besides, I have a lot of studying to do, and I can use some quiet time on the desk. . . . So I follow Mr. Morghan's rule: Act friendly but don't get friendly."

"Lenny!" his mother shouted from the kitchen. "If you're gonna gab instead of studyin' your books, get off your rusty dusty and help me with dinner!"

Lenny jumped up and grinned. "Gotta go!"

THURSDAY, SEPTEMBER 10—*The early bird gets the worm.*

At six o'clock Qwilleran picked up Polly in Indian Village for the drive to West Middle Hummock, where the Lanspeaks had their country estate. His first words were, "Did you get the ring?"

"It's breathtaking! I can't believe that it's mine—or will be after December 25."

"Nonsense! Start wearing it now. Where is it?"

"I went directly to the bank and put it in my lock-box. But I can't wait for you to see it!"

"How was the appointment with Old Campo?"

"All business. No hand-kissing or compliments. I declined a cup of tea and kept looking at my watch. They showed me the ring, and I handed over the cash."

"Did they count it?"

"The assistant took it into the other room. I'm sure she counted it."

Qwilleran said, "Both you and I must avoid any slip of the tongue that would reveal my presence at the tea."

West Middle Hummock was an exclusive enclave of country estates, and the landscape was a panorama of woods and meadows, winding roads bordered with wild-flowers, and rustic bridges over gurgling streams.

"Isn't it lovely?" Polly murmured.

"Would you like to live here?"

"No, but I like to visit once in a while. Carol is preparing dinner; it's her cook's night off."

The Lanspeaks lived in an unpretentious farmhouse furnished with country antiques that looked like museum quality. When their children were young, they had kept a family cow, riding horses, and a few chickens and ducks. Now Carol and Larry were alone —except for the couple who took care of the housekeeping and grounds—and they concentrated on running the department store and participating in the theatre club, historical society, genealogy club, and gourmet group.

Larry met them on the front steps, saying, "The visiting firemen will be a little late, so we'll start the Happy Hour without them. Old Campo doesn't drink, anyway."

Uh-huh, Qwilleran thought.

Carol came out of the kitchen, where she was preparing her famous breast of duck with prosciutto and mushroom duxelles.

Qwilleran asked, "Has this year's Delacamp expedition been a success so far?"

"He never discusses that aspect of his visit," Carol said, "but I know that Mrs. Woodinghurst sold her famous brooch yesterday, and he's agreed to take Maggie Sprenkle's torsade."

They talked in chummy fashion about the Tuesday Tea, and Qwilleran entertained them with an account of his discomforts and boredom as a security guard. Then the honored guests arrived, and the mood became formal. What happened next is best described in Qwilleran's own words, which he recorded in his personal journal:

This guy Delacamp has been coming up here for more than twenty years and is not on first-name terms with anyone—even Carol and Larry. His niece was introduced as Ms. North. "Pamela," she said shyly, keeping her eyes cast down. Could this be the chick who pestered Lenny Inchpot at the reception desk in the late hours? She was wearing her tailored suit, and her uncle wore a blazer obviously tailored to flatter his expanding girth.

He said to me, "Haven't we met in the last few days? At the country club perhaps?" I professed regret at not having had the pleasure, but I began to wonder if my disguise had been less effective than Carol insisted.

Quickly she said, "Mr. Qwilleran writes a column for the newspaper, and his picture appears at the head of it. That's the answer."

Unconvinced, Old Campo continued to throw glances in my direction all evening. He asked for a cup of tea when Larry was ready to serve a second round of drinks, leading me to challenge him. "As a journalist and a confirmed coffee-drinker, may I ask why you prefer tea?"

"Tea is the thinking man's coffee," he began. "For five thousand years in China it has been known as a revitalizing beverage, increasing concentration and alertness. Later, the Japanese promoted harmony and tranquillity with the tea ceremony. Dutch and Portuguese traders introduced tea to England and Russia. Caravans of two or three hundred camels used to bring chests of tea to the Russian border. Clipper ships raced each other from China to London."

His niece was yawning. She spoke only when spoken to but paid deferential attention to Old Campo. At one point she whispered to him, and he said, "Now I know where I've seen you! In my suite there's a portrait of Mark Twain. You could be brothers!"

During Carol's excellent dinner he discussed the three thousand kinds of tea in the world, and then the seven grades of tea. The latter sounded like a comic routine, and I was glad I had my miniature tape recorder in my pocket when he recited them: Pekoe, orange pekoe, flowery orange pekoe, golden flowery orange pekoe, tippy golden flowery orange pekoe, finest tippy golden flowery orange pekoe, and special finest tippy golden flowery orange pekoe.

The after-dinner tea was Darjeeling, "the champagne of teas," we were told. "Grown in India in the Himalayan foothills. Sometimes on a forty-five-degree slope."

The special guests left shortly after that, and the rest of us had some good strong coffee while we recapped the evening and had a few laughs.

At one point Polly excused herself and returned with a look of wonderment. "Carol! You've done over the powder room! It's spectacular!"

Naturally, Nosy Me had to investigate. They had made one entire wall into a lighted niche with glass shelves for a collection of French perfume bottles.

"Larry gives me perfume on every anniversary," she said, "and I save the bottles: Shalimar, Champs Elyseés, L'Heure Bleue—all the Guerlain classics. The bottles are works of art. Every time we go to Paris I haunt the antique shops and flea markets for vintage bottles. Some are priced as high as five thousand francs—and more if they're Baccarat."

Little did Polly know I had special-ordered a bottle of L'Heure Bleue for her.

As Qwilleran and Polly drove back to Indian Village, she said, "Mr. Delacamp is visiting Maggie tomorrow morning to buy her pearl-and-diamond torsade. I'd love to know what he offers for it. I won't ask, of course, and Maggie won't tell."

"And even if she does, she isn't bound to tell the truth. You know the old rule: *Ask me no questions, and I'll tell you no lies.* Who said that? Shakespeare?"

"Oliver Goldsmith," she corrected him. "And he said 'fibs'—not 'lies.' It was a line in *She Stoops to Conquer*."

"With a friend like you, Polly, who needs an encyclopedia?"

"Thank you, dear. That's the nicest thing you ever

said! Did you know that 'fib' has been a euphemism for 'lie' as far back as the eighteenth century? It's derived from 'fibble-fabble.' I hope I'm not boring you."

"Not at all. This is a lot more interesting than tea."

Conversation stopped as they passed the site of the Old Glory mine and turned to look at the old shafthouse, a spectral presence in the moonlight. Then she said, "I hear the historical society and the county commissioners are squabbling about the new historical markers—to put them outside the fence, inside the fence, or on the fence. What's your opinion, Qwill?"

"Inside the fence. They're bronze and susceptible to theft."

"Down Below, perhaps, but not up here."

"There are vacationers from Down Below who might like to take home a bronze souvenir. I still say it's safest to post it inside the fence."

A quarter mile rolled by, and he said, "Tomorrow afternoon I visit Maggie to tape her great-grandmother's story."

"Take an oxygen inhaler," she advised. "Her apartment is suffocatingly Victorian. But you'll like her late husband's collection of books."

"Eddington Smith sold me a fine old copy of *Oedipus Rex* this week. Handsome binding but poor translation."

"In Canada this summer I saw a wonderful production of the play, complete with grotesque masks and exaggerated buskins."

They turned into Ittibittiwassee Road. He asked, "How did you like Carol's breast of duck?"

"It was a little rich for my taste."

"But the blackberry cobbler was good."

When they reached Indian Village Polly asked, "Would you like to come in and say goodnight to Brutus and Catta?"

"For a few minutes."

It was late when Qwilleran returned to the barn that night, and the internal clocks of the Siamese told them their bedtime snack was long overdue. Yum Yum prowled aimlessly; Koko sat on his haunches, his tail slapping the floor impatiently. They gave the impression they were too weak from hunger to protest; that was one of their subtle strategies, designed to make him feel guilty.

"Sorry about this, but you know how it is," he apologized while measuring a serving of Kabibbles on each plate. "We had breast of duck. I had hoped to bring you a taste, but there was none left."

After that they were ready to sleep. He escorted them up to their lodgings on the top balcony and said goodnight, leaving their door open. They never prowled in the night like feral cats; they had adapted to the human sleep schedule. But they often liked to rise at dawn and watch the early birds getting their worms. On the main floor there were windows with excellent views and accommodatingly wide sills.

During the night an unnatural sound disturbed Qwilleran's sleep. He was dreaming about the Wild West and a coyote howling on a distant peak. He always dreamed graphically, and a coyote was an appropriate part of the scenario. Yet, the howl grew louder and closer and more urgent. He sat up in bed and took a moment to adjust to reality: barn . . . Pickax . . . cats . . .

Koko was howling outside his bedroom door! Was it an alarm? A warning? Qwilleran threw the master switch that illuminated the premises, indoors and out, and went to investigate. He found nothing wrong, no prowlers, not even a waddling raccoon.

As for the cat, he had returned to his quarters and was asleep in his basket. Perhaps he had been dreaming, too, Qwilleran thought. He looked at his bedside clock. It was two-thirty.

six

Friday, September 11—*When elephants fight, it's the grass that suffers.*

After the unexplained disturbance in the night, Qwilleran had to sit up and read for a while to relax his nerves. Consequently he was still sleeping when a morning phone call made a rude interruption. He answered the bedside phone with a single syllable resembling a grunt.

"Sorry, Qwill," said a woman's wide-awake voice. "Am I calling too early? It's going on eight-thirty!" She, of course, was dressed, breakfasted, and ready to leave for work at the library.

Groggily, Qwilleran explained, "Koko had a stomach ache in the night and kept me awake, so I had to sleep in. Does Brutus ever howl in the middle of the night?"

"No, but he's not as vocal as Koko. . . . All I wanted, Qwill, was to ask what we're wearing to dinner in the

Mackintosh Room tomorrow night. We don't want to overdo the 'bonnie Scots' idea, do we?"

"Right you are. No kilts. No tartans."

"I thought my olive-green silk would be good with the plaid chair seats and green carpet."

"Sounds okay. I'll wear a gray tweed jacket to go with my gray tweed moustache." Qwilleran was beginning to wake up.

"I'm working tomorrow, so I'll go home to dress and then ride into town with the Rikers."

"Good idea."

"I'm really excited about the dinner. Did you read Mildred's interview with Chef Wingo on yesterday's food page? It was inspiring! . . . Do I hear Koko making a commotion?"

"Yes, he's ordering his breakfast: ham and eggs with a side order of American fries."

"Go back to bed! You're not ready," Polly said.

Qwilleran slipped into a jumpsuit before opening his bedroom door and following two caterwauling cats down the ramp. Instead of going to the feeding station, however, Koko jumped on the library table and put one paw on the phone.

It's going to ring, Qwilleran thought, and before he could press the button on the automated coffeemaker, it rang. In an agreeable tone with a rising inflection he said, "Good morning?"

The solemn voice of the attorney answered. "Qwill, this is Bart. Prepare for some shocking news!"

Qwilleran hesitated. He was thinking, The hotel's bombed again.

"Qwill, are you there? Delacamp died in his sleep last night!"

"I can't believe it! I had dinner with him at the Lanspeaks'. He was in fine form, although he left early. Was it a heart attack?"

"I don't know. The doctor is on the way to the inn. I'm at home. Barry Morghan called me here."

"Did his niece find him? She must be vastly upset."

"I don't have any details. But I thought you ought to know that all deals are off."

"I'll phone Carol, and she can notify those who had appointments pending. Too bad, isn't it?"

"Yes, too bad."

Qwilleran phoned the newspaper first.

Then he called the Lanspeak house in West Middle Hummock. The housekeeper said that Mister and Missus had left for downtown; he called the store; they had not yet arrived. While his hand hovered over the receiver in a spasm of indecision, a call came in from Barry Morghan, speaking in a hollow voice.

"Qwill! Bad news!"

"I know. Bart phoned. Delacamp is dead."

"Yes, but . . . the coroner is here, and it looks bad! The police are all over the place. Half the third floor is sealed off. . . . I can't talk now. Would you notify Bart of the situation?" The phone clicked unceremoniously.

First Qwilleran called the paper with the latest tip.

Then he phoned the attorney.

His wife said, "He's just driving out—"

"*Catch him!*"

He visualized her running after the car, screaming and waving her arms.

"Caught him!" she gasped after a few minutes.

Her husband was less perturbed. "What's up?"

"It's worse than we thought, Bart. They obviously suspect homicide."

"Jewel thieves?"

"Sounds like it, doesn't it?" Qwilleran agreed.

"We were assured that the jewels and large amounts of cash would be brought to the safe in the manager's office every night."

"Something went wrong."

"I'll go right to the inn. I may be needed. Thanks, Qwill."

Qwilleran felt a rush of blood, a burst of energy, a flashback to his old days as a police reporter Down Below. Koko, who had been sitting there to monitor the calls, was less involved. He pushed the script of the theatre club's new play onto the floor.

"Not now," Qwilleran said, picking it up and putting it in a safe place. He was asking himself: Where was the niece? What could she tell? When had she last seen the jewel cases? What had been done with the cash from the day's purchasers? After leaving the dinner party early, where had they gone? What did they do? . . . And then his curiosity took a different turn: Why did Koko howl in the middle of the night? It was about two-thirty. What was the time of death? And why was the cat sitting near the phone, looking so wise?

No doubt about it, Qwilleran mused; he was an unusual animal. All cats have certain senses that are denied to humans; they tell time without a clock and find their way without a map. Koko's intuition went beyond that. He knew right from wrong, and he had known that something was wrong at two-thirty A.M. Some things cannot be explained, and Qwilleran had learned to accept the cat's uncanny perceptions.

His own curiosity about the murder would have to go unsatisfied; no facts were known. Even WPKX had nothing to offer when the first news bulletin interrupted the country music:

"A Chicago businessman registered at the Mackintosh Inn was found dead in the presidential suite this morning, a victim of homicide. No further details have been released, and the victim's name is withheld until the notification of relatives. Local and state police are investigating."

Qwilleran was aware that his newspaper would have reporters out in the field, hounding every news source in time for the noon deadline and afternoon publication. Still, he felt the urge to do a little snooping himself. He dressed hurriedly and walked downtown, without even saying goodbye to the Siamese—a courtesy that meant more to himself than to them.

His first stop was the public library, known as the information center of the county—not because of its extensive book collection and expensive computer system but because it was the hub of the Pickax grapevine. In moments of crisis its subscribers flocked to the library to exchange questions, hearsay, and rash guesses, all of which would be circulated throughout the county by

phone, in coffee shops, and on street corners. It was a traditional system that worked—for better or worse.

Qwilleran walked slowly up the broad steps to the library, wondering what information and misinformation
would be circulating at this early hour. He found the
young clerks behind the desk in a huddle, speaking in
hushed voices. Volunteers had their heads together in
the stacks. Subscribers stood about in clusters, their
solemn faces indicating they were not critiquing a best-
seller. Only Mac and Katie, the two feline mascots, were
unperturbed, being engaged in social grooming. Qwilleran spoke to them, and they looked up at him briefly
with extended tongues. Then he bounded up the stairs to
the mezzanine, where Polly could be seen in her glass-
enclosed cubicle.

She was hanging up the phone as he entered. "Well!"
she said vehemently. "Have you heard the news?"

"Off-putting, isn't it?" he remarked. "You and I and
the Lanspeaks must have been the last outside contacts
he had! How did you hear about it?"

"One of our volunteers has a son who's a day porter at
the inn. She knew I'd met Mr. Delacamp."

"Did her son have any particulars?"

"Only that the assistant hadn't been around—probably upstairs being interrogated. It sounds ominous,
doesn't it? What's your mission this morning?"

"I'm on my way to see the Lanspeaks at the store."

"Carol will be flabbergasted!"

At the department store he went directly to the office
under the main staircase, standing outside until she had
finished a phone call.

She beckoned to him to come in, but all she could say was, "I'm flabbergasted!"

He sat down without waiting to be invited. "How did you hear about it?"

"From Viyella, the morning clerk at the inn. She's in my Sunday school class and was one of the French maids at the tea. She knew I'd be flabbergasted."

"Aren't we all?"

"Do you have any inside information?"

"Only that the police are there, and half the third floor is cordoned off."

"Viyella says they're questioning the staff and the guests and cautioning everyone not to talk about the case."

"How did she contact you?"

"She wrote a note, and the day porter brought it to me."

"What's Larry's reaction to the news?"

"He doesn't know! I drove him to the airport this morning, and he boarded the eight o'clock shuttle to Minneapolis. There's a merchandising show there, and he won't be back until tomorrow night. I'll phone him, of course. Wait till he hears! He has always had a jealous-husband theory, you know." She stifled a slight giggle. "At least we know it wasn't Mr. Woodinghurst. He died twenty years ago."

Qwilleran said, "Just because it happened here, it doesn't follow that the perpetrator was a local."

"You're so right, Qwill! I'd prefer to think it's an outside job."

"What effect will it have on his customers?"

"Those who wanted to buy tomorrow will be disappointed, of course, but I'm concerned about the Old Guard who were expecting to sell to him today. Some of them really need the money. They're old-timers who thought they were financially set for life. Then along came inflation and dishonest relatives and bad investment advice. It's sad. They should be notified, in case they don't hear it on the radio, but his niece has the schedule. The poor girl must be terribly upset."

Qwilleran next went to Lois's Luncheonette for the mid-morning coffee klatsch, where caffeine addicts and assorted loafers met to exchange opinions and rumors about current events. Everyone had a connection to the grapevine—a son-in-law or neighbor or fellow worker who knew the inside story. Lois, whose son was captain of the inn's desk clerks, had a direct line to the facts.

"They called him a Chicago businessman on the air," she announced while bustling around with the coffee server, "but everybody knows he was a jeweler with a million dollars' worth of stuff in his luggage."

"They didn't say nothin' about his girl! Where's his girl?"

"Prob'ly took off with the killer and the loot."

"Coulda been kidnapped. He was her uncle."

Lois said, "Yeah . . . well . . . Lenny says she was no niece."

"Her and the killer were in cahoots, if you ask me. Somebody from Chicago."

"'Tain't fair! Strangers come up here and get themselves knocked off, and it makes us look bad."

"Why'd it happen just when we got a nice new hotel and some good publicity? Makes me madder'n a wet hen!"

"Eleven o'clock! Turn on the news!"

Lois switched on the radio that occupied a shelf above the cash register, and her customers heard one additional scrap of news:

"The State Bureau of Investigation has been called in to assist local police in the investigation of a homicide. A Chicago businessman . . ."

Qwilleran paid for his coffee and went home, taking time to walk through the inn's parking lot. Delacamp's Mercedes rental car was still there.

When Qwilleran turned the key in the back-door lock, he heard the welcoming chorus indoors and realized once more how much he appreciated his housemates. He had lived alone for most of his adult life—before adopting Koko and Yum Yum. They were companionable, handsome, entertaining—and admirably independent. Sometimes exasperatingly so.

One of the pleasures they shared was reading aloud. He had a good voice, having trained to be an actor before switching to journalism. When he read aloud from the vintage books that filled his shelves, he dramatized the prose in a way that excited his listeners. Currently they were reading the play-script of *Night Must Fall:* the smarmy lines of the houseboy, the petulant fussiness of Mrs. Bramson, and the country dialects of the kitchen help.

They had reached Scene Four. Yum Yum was curled

contentedly on Qwilleran's lap: Koko perched on the
back of his chair, looking over his shoulder as if following the printed words, purring in his ear or tickling his
neck with twitching whiskers. Mrs. Bramson was worry-
ing about her jewel box. Danny was being overly attentive. . . . Suddenly he picked up a cushion and smothered
his rich employer.

"YOW!" came a piercing howl in Qwilleran's ear.

"Please!" the man protested, putting a hand to his ear.
"Don't do that!" But then he felt a sensation on his upper
lip, and he tamped his moustache. It was always the
source of his hunches. Now he knew—or thought he
knew—more about the murder than the investigators
had revealed.

The Friday edition of the *Moose County Something*
would have the latest—at two o'clock. At one-thirty
Qwilleran had an appointment with Maggie Sprenkle.

The Sprenkle Building, across Main Street from
the Mackintosh Inn, was a stone structure like all
the others downtown, and its history dated back to the
days when merchants always lived "over the store." Now
the storefronts on the ground floor had been updated
into offices for an insurance agency and a realty firm. At
one side a door led up to Maggie's palace on the second
and third floors.

Qwilleran rang the bell, waited for the buzzer to un-
lock the door, and found himself in a steep, narrow stair-
well. It seemed narrower and steeper because of the thick
stair carpet in a pattern of roses and the velvety rose-
pink walls hung with dozens of old engravings.

Maggie was waiting at the top. "Hang on to the handrail," she cautioned. "The stairs are murder! Most of my guests come in the back, where there's an elevator."

"That's all right," he called up the stairs. "I prefer the dramatic approach."

He made it safely to the top, and she welcomed him with a bear hug.

He found himself in a two-story foyer with a skylight and another staircase leading to the upper level. This reception area also functioned as a library, its shelves glowing with the polished calf bindings of fine old books.

"Do you have any Mark Twain?" he asked, thinking to introduce an earthy note.

"Yes, indeed!" she replied in her usual hearty manner. "My grandfather-in-law entertained Mr. Clemens when he lectured here. . . . Come into the parlor. The ladies are waiting to meet you."

For a moment he expected the ladies of the library's board of directors, forgetting Sarah, Charlotte, Carrie, Flora, and Louisa May. They sat in the five windows: a tiger with white boots and bib, a calico, an orange marmalade, a black and-white, and a snowy white with blue eyes. Each had her own windowsill and sat under a canopy of lace curtain, cut away at the bottom for easy access.

"Good afternoon, ladies," he said.

All but the white one turned away from their pigeon-watching and gave him an inquisitive glance.

"Charlotte is deaf," Maggie explained, "but she's an adorable little creature."

"Unusual curtains," he remarked.

"Amanda Goodwinter had them custom-made in Belgium. She's done all my decorating for forty years. Wonderful woman! And now she's going to run for mayor, and we must all support her. . . . Do sit down, and I'll bring the tea tray."

"I'd rather walk around and ogle your collection," he said. "It's a museum!"

The rosy velvet walls of the parlor were hung floor-to-ceiling with old oil paintings in ornate frames. Furniture crowded the room: heavy carved tables with marble tops; button-tufted chairs and settees heaped with needlepoint pillows; lamps with hand-painted globes; and everywhere a clutter of crystal and porcelain bric-a-brac.

When Maggie returned with the tea, she said, "Did you know that Florence Nightingale had sixty cats? Not all at once, of course. And she named them after famous personalities: Disraeli, Mr. Gladstone, and so forth. . . . All my ladies have come from the animal shelter where I work as a volunteer."

They sat in carved side chairs at a carved table, and tea was poured into small porcelain cups with finger-trap handles, but—for Qwilleran—a plate of chocolate brownies made it all worthwhile.

"Polly said they're your favorite sweet," Maggie said. "She's such a wonderful woman! And I'm so glad she has you for a friend."

"It's my good fortune," he murmured.

Maggie chattered on: about the controversy over the library's bookmobile . . . about the failing health of Osmond Hasselrich, senior partner of the city's most prestigious law firm . . . about the Scottish Gathering. "Polly tells me that you and she are going on Sunday."

"Yes. Polly likes the piping and dancing. I'll attend the

athletic events with Whannell MacWhannell on Saturday."

"Wonderful man!" she said. "He handles my tax work."

She had not said a word about the murder. Yet it was generally known that she intended to sell the fabulous Sprenkle necklace to the jeweler. It was a strange oversight, considering local passion for commenting on the latest news.

As for Qwilleran, he was there for another purpose. After declining a third chocolate brownie, he drew a tape recorder from a pocket and said, "Now let's hear the story about your great-grandmother, Maggie."

"Do you want to ask me questions?"

"No, just repeat what you told the genealogical club."

Maggie's tale was later transcribed as follows:

This story about pioneer days in Moose County has been handed down in my family and I believe it to be absolutely true. There were heroes and villains in our history, and many of them were involved in mining.

As you know, there were ten mines in operation—and enough coal for all—but most of the owners were greedy, exploiting their workers shamefully. My great-grandfather, Patrick Borleston, owned the Big B mine. He and another owner, Seth Dimsdale, cared about their workers' health, safety, and families, and their attitude paid off in loyalty and productivity. Their competitors were envious to the point of hostility. When Patrick was killed in a carriage accident, his workers were convinced that someone had purposely spooked his horses.

They suspected Ned Bucksmith, owner of the Buckshot mine. Immediately he tried to buy the Big B from the widow. But Bridget was a strong woman. She said she'd operate it herself. The idea of a woman mine operator shocked the other owners, and when the mother of three proceeded to do a man's job better than they could, their antagonism grew—especially that of Ned Bucksmith. She was twice his size, being tall, buxom, and broad-shouldered. She always wore a long, voluminous black dress with a little white lace collar and a pancake hat tied under her chin with ribbons.

Folks said it was the lace collar and ribbons that sent Ned Bucksmith over the edge. He and the other mine owners met in the back room of the K Saloon on Thursday evenings to drink whiskey and play cards, and he got them plotting against Big Bridget. One Thursday night a window was broken in the shack she used for an office. The next week a giant tree was felled across her access road. Next her night watchman put out a fire that could have burned down the office.

One Thursday morning Bridget was sitting at her roll-top desk when she heard a frantic banging on the door. There on the doorstep was a young boy, out of breath from running. "Them men!" he gasped. "At the saloon. They be blowin' up your mine!" Then he dashed away.

That evening Bridget went to the saloon in her tent-like black dress and pancake hat, carrying a shotgun. She barged in, knocked over a few chairs, and shouted, "Where are those dirty rats?" Customers hid under tables as she swept toward the back room. "Who's gonna blow up my mine?" she thundered and pointed the gun at Ned Bucksmith. He went out the window headfirst, and the other men piled out the back door. She followed them and unloaded a few warning shots.

There was no more trouble at the Big B. Now if you're wondering about the youngster who tipped her off, he was Ned Bucksmith's boy, and he had a crush on Bridget's daughter. When they grew up, they were married, and that young boy became my grandfather.

Qwilleran turned off his tape recorder. "You tell the story well, Maggie."

"That's how I told it at the genealogy club. One man came up afterward and said his ancestors knew Bridget. They worked for her."

"It must be gratifying to know who your forebears are. I never knew my grandparents. How do you know details like the lace collar and pancake hat?"

"The historical society has a daguerreotype of her. She looks like a king-size Queen Victoria."

"You've inherited some of her fine qualities, Maggie."

"And some of Bucksmith's bad ones. That was my maiden name, and I was glad to get rid of it when I married Mr. Sprenkle. He was a gentleman and a gentle man. He grew prize roses. Do you like the roses in this carpet? They remind me of him. Have another brownie, Qwill."

"You talked me into it. By the way, I think the Big B shafthouse is the most dramatic."

"They say it has a subterranean lake at the bottom of the shaft."

Qwilleran walked to the window to say goodbye to the ladies and look at the windows of the inn. He said, "There was a murder in that room on the third floor early this morning."

"I know. Poor Mr. Delacamp! He was kind of silly, but we liked him. He was supposed to make me an offer for the Sprenkle torsade today." She shrugged. "Perhaps I'll have it made into five collars for my ladies. . . . Incidentally, Qwill, I saw something last night, and I'm wondering if I should report it to the police."

"It depends what it was."

"Well, Carrie was unwell, and I was sitting up with her—just to make her feel cared for and loved. We sat in the dark. It was late, and there were no lights in any of the guestrooms across the street. The windows have those narrow-slat blinds, you know, and suddenly I saw streaks of light behind the blinds in two of the windows on the third floor—like the beams of a flashlight moving around."

"How long did the light show last?"

"Only a minute or two."

"It wouldn't hurt to report it," Qwilleran said. "You never know if some small observation will develop into a clue. Do you know what time it was?"

"Well, the bars close at two, and there's a brief rush of traffic, and then it's quiet. About two-thirty, I'd say."

"Do you know anyone at the police department?"

"Andrew Brodie—I know him very well. He played the bagpipe at Mr. Sprenkle's funeral."

. . .

When Qwilleran left the Sprenkle building he crossed the street to pick up Friday's paper in the lobby of the inn, and he was disappointed to find that the *Something* knew of no more about the murder than did WPKX. He did, however, see Roger MacGillivray in the parking lot. "Are you on the Delacamp story?" Qwilleran asked him.

"I was, but they're not releasing any more details. I'm on my way to cover a meeting of the Interact Club at the school."

Knowing that reporters always know more than they're at liberty to write, he asked, "Any off-the-record dope on the girl?"

"She's gone, but her clothes and things are still in her room, and the rental car's still here on the lot. And here's the twist: The jewel cases are still in the manager's safe. Figure that!"

"Why are the authorities being so cagey?"

"The PPD is waiting for the SBI to release information."

"Do you know the time and cause of death?"

"Oh, sure. Suffocation, probably with a bed pillow. Between two and three A.M."

seven

SATURDAY, SEPTEMBER 12—*To a man with a rifle, everything looks like a squirrel.*

As Qwilleran watched the Siamese gobble their breakfast and then groom themselves in the age-old style practiced by felines around the world, he shook his head in wonder. Here were two cats doing what cats do, and yet . . . one of them had yowled officiously when a character in the play was suffocated with a pillow! Something had clicked in his little brain, connecting the drama with the real-life incident at the inn. There was no doubt about it: Koko was gifted with a rare intellect.

Sitting in the kitchen observing the grooming ritual, Qwilleran asked himself, What does Koko have that other cats do not? The answer was: sixty whiskers, eyebrows included, and counting both sides of his noble head. His reverie was interrupted by the telephone, which seemed to be ringing more urgently than usual.

Polly was on the line, speaking with the breathlessness of one who is late for work.

"Any news about the murder?"

"Only rumors," he mumbled, still lost in his own profound thoughts about Koko.

"Well, I have something to report. Didn't have time to call you last night. Bird Club, you know. Exciting meeting!"

"I'll bet, he thought. "What's your news?"

"The police came to the library yesterday, to talk to me."

Qwilleran snapped to attention. "About what?"

"About the purchase of my ring. They had the appointment book with a list of prospective purchasers. They knew I was interested in a ring for seven-ninety-five. They wanted to know if I'd bought it with credit card, personal check, or bank check. When I said the jeweler required cash, the officer's Adam's apple wobbled."

"Mine wobbled, too," Qwilleran admitted, "when I first heard about the cash-only policy. Was he embezzling from his firm or defrauding the government?"

"I must hang up now and go to the library. See you tonight. Enjoy the games!"

Whannell MacWhannell called for Qwilleran at the barn, and they drove to the fairgrounds in the accountant's car. Both men were in Highland dress: kilts, sporrans, knee-hose, garters with flashes, brogues, white sports shirts, and Glengarry caps tilted rakishly over the right eyebrow. And it must be said that both men had the commanding stature and swagger to carry it off.

Big Mac's first words were predictable: "I can't believe it! I can't believe the new inn opened with a murder! I never met Delacamp, but I was always aware of the social and economic waves he made during his visits. But why now? And why here?"

"Times are changing—even in Pickax," Qwilleran muttered.

"Jewel thieves are the prime suspects, I suppose," said the accountant with a chuckle, "but I have a client who would qualify for the honor. Five years ago his wife drew ten thousand from their joint bank account and bought some earrings."

"I suppose you know purchasers have to pay in hard currency."

Big Mac chuckled again. "Can't you picture the local ladies lined up at the teller's window with suitcases and shopping bags to fill with twenties? Plenty of folks in the north country don't recognize anything larger than a twenty as negotiable."

It was the first time Qwilleran had attended a Scottish Gathering and the first time one had been held in Moose County. Bixby County usually excelled in athletic events, and Lockmaster in music and dance. This year the idea of a local venue had charged Moose Countians with the will to win.

There was more to the annual Scottish Gathering than competition, of course. It was a gathering of clans, a renewal of friendships, a scene of festivity. There were crowds of happy celebrators, Scottish food and drink, hospitality tents in bold colors, pennants flapping in the breeze, fiddlers fiddling, bagpipers piping.

Qwilleran and Big Mac pushed through the crowds to an open field where a sheep-herding demonstration was scheduled. A flock of a dozen sheep was being unloaded from a stake-truck belonging to the Ogilvie Ranch and herded into a temporary corral divided into a maze of miniature pastures. The shepherd was Buster Ogilvie himself, carrying a crooked staff. Qwilleran knew the whole family. The shepherd grew the wool; his wife spun it into yarn; their daughter knitted it into sweaters and socks.

"From ewe to you!" the Ogilvies quipped.

A crowd had gathered, and Ogilvie made an announcement in the relaxed, gentle manner typical of persons who deal with sheep: "Folks, we've brought a five-year-old Border collie to show you how he does his job. The breed was developed many centuries ago on the border between Scotland and England. This breed of dog is not only intelligent but born with the sheep-herding instinct. Also, they're workaholics. Here's . . . Duncan!"

A rough-coated black-and-white dog with tail carried low came bounding from the truck cab, right on cue. He went directly to the penned sheep, rounded them up in businesslike fashion, and herded them into the next small pasture. They moved obediently and placidly in a close-order cluster of woolly backs.

Ogilvie said, "You'll notice that Duncan doesn't yap or make a fuss. He doesn't have to. They know what he wants them to do. Even rebellious sheep obey him. If something happens to make the flock nervous, Duncan can calm them down just by being there."

By the time the sheep had scattered in the second enclosure, Duncan rounded them up and herded them into a third.

Big Mac muttered to Qwilleran, "The poor devils must be all confused."

"They're sheep. Theirs not to question why."

Ogilvie said, "There's a silent understanding between a Border collie and his flock. Some folks call it magic. It's a kind of mental telepathy. I think he reads my mind, too. . . . Now, in case you're wondering about all this herding, we have to move the flock from one pasture to another to give them a balanced diet, as well as periods of shade and water. If sheep gorge too much, they can get bloated, and that can be fatal."

Briskly and with authority Duncan moved his willing charges through the maze and back to the starting place. Watchers applauded, cameras clicked, and he trotted back to the truck.

"Good show!" Qwilleran said to the shepherd. "He's a real pro!"

Big Mac said, "I wouldn't mind having a dog like that."

"That's the problem," Ogilvie said. "The Borders are so friendly that people want them for pets, but that's not fair to the dog and not fair to the breed. You see, for hundreds of years they've been bred as working dogs, and if they don't get enough work, they're frustrated. There's a story—whether it's true or not, I can't guarantee—but it's about a Border collie living on a farm where they didn't give him enough work to do. One day he trotted down the road to the next farm, rounded up their chickens, geese, hogs, and goats, and herded them back to his own farm."

The food tents were offering mutton pies, fried herring cakes, bridies, and assorted sweets such as scones and shortbread. Qwilleran and Big Mac chose the bridies, a kind of meat-filled pastry turnover similar to Moose County's Cornish pasties but without the potato. They carried their repast to a picnic table and were bantering with Scots from Bixby when Lois Inchpot walked past their table and pointed a threatening finger at them.

"You guys get out there in the bleachers and root for my boy, do you hear? He's in the footraces, starting in a few minutes."

Big Mac mumbled, "We'd better do what she says, or we'll never get a second cup of coffee—free. Personally I prefer the heavy games to the races, although I know it's traditional for Scots to respect speed. In the early days of clan warfare they needed fast runners as messengers as well as strong men for bodyguards."

They went to the bleachers and roared encouragement to Lenny, while his mother stood up and waved her arms like a middle-aged cheerleader. In spite of their support he never came in better than third. Bike racing, not foot-racing, was his strong suit.

The big men who next paraded around the field were no candidates for Mr. America's crown; they were just big, beefy heavyweights—some in kilts, some in shorts. All wore extra-extra-large T-shirts stretched tightly across their torsos. The logos on the shirts were an eight-point buck (Moose County), a raging bull (Bixby), and Pegasus (Lockmaster).

"What I'd like to see," said Big Mac, "is the test of strength and grit called Hauling the Bucket, but it's probably been outlawed. A guy picks up two iron buckets weighing a couple of hundred pounds apiece, and he runs—or struggles—down the track until he's forced to drop them. The longest run wins. As the saying goes, if you don't drop dead, you haven't been trying hard enough."

"What I want to see is called Tossing the Caber," Qwilleran said. "Lenny says there's quite a trick to it, and there's a desk clerk at the inn who's mastered the trick."

The program listed five events, involving tossing, pitching, throwing, putting, and heaving.

1. Throwing the Hammer. It was four feet long and weighed twenty pounds. The thrower stood with back to the goal and his feet planted firmly on the ground. Then he twirled and let it fly, his kilt swirling in a circle of pleats. A Bixby contender won handily.
2. Heaving the Sheaf. A burlap sack filled with twenty pounds of hay had to be lifted with a three-pronged pitchfork and pitched over a crossbar that started at eighteen feet from the ground. It was another win for the raging bulls.
3. Putting the Stone. The contestant had to balance a sixteen-pound stone ball with one hand at shoulder height, then heave it. Another win for Bixby.

4. Throwing the Box. A fifty-six-pound box-weight with ring attached had to be flung over a bar. Moose County won but only by default when the leading Bixby contender ran afoul of the rules.

5. Tossing the Caber. This feat was performed with a twenty-foot cedar log weighing more than a hundred pounds, and it required skill as well as strength.

A number of big men took the field for the caber toss, but Moose County's Boze Campbell was the most formidable.

"He's the desk clerk," Qwilleran told Big Mac. "A woodsman by trade. A latter-day Paul Bunyan, from what I hear."

One by one the contenders tossed the pole in the air, hoping it would land at "twelve o'clock." If it soared and then fell flat, the crowd would groan "Aw-w-w!" It was supposed to flip end-over-end in midair. That was the art! Each man had three tries.

To Qwilleran there was something suspenseful about the caber toss. He had his camera ready, and he snapped pictures of the entire ritual: Boze swaggering onto the field . . . Lenny saying something in his ear . . . Boze taking a confident stance at the end of the pole that lay on the ground. An official stood at the other end, facing Boze—then picked up his end and "walked it" hand-over-hand to an upright position. Boze was squatting with feet wide apart as the pole was leaned against his shoulder. He concentrated. With fingers interlocked he hoisted it to vertical. The crowd was silent as it balanced precariously. Then Boze ran awkwardly forward a few paces before tossing the caber. It soared! It flipped end over end! It landed as close to twelve o'clock as could be imagined.

Three times Boze accomplished the incredible feat, and the crowd surged onto the field, cheering and whooping, and Boze's teammates lifted him to their shoulders. Photographers from all three county newspapers scurried about. The hero wore a bland smile.

"Historic event!" said Big Mac.

"Front page news," said Qwilleran.

"Let's get out of here before the Bixby crowd riots."

"They won't. The sheriff's dog is here, and his mere presence keeps the rowdies under control."

He had to go home and dress for dinner. Big Mac had to attend a business meeting of the curling club, of which he was treasurer. "Are you interested in curling, Qwill?"

"You mean, that sport where they slide big stones around a rink and sweep the ice furiously with little brooms?"

"Something of that sort."

"It's an old man's game."

"Not any more! It's for all ages, male and female. It has Olympic status, requiring skill. And it's a social sport."

"How social can you be in temperatures below freezing?"

"We play on an indoor rink."

"Well, I might be available," Qwilleran said, "if you need a broomkeeper."

A delegation of three from Indian Village—Polly and the Rikers—arrived at the barn at six-thirty and trooped through the back door into the kitchen with the nonchalance of frequent visitors.

Qwilleran asked, "Shall we have a libation before we go to the inn? Our reservation is for seven-thirty."

"I'll have the usual," said Arch.

"The usual," Mildred said.

"The usual," Polly echoed.

While the drinks were being prepared, Polly filled the nut bowls, and the Rikers strolled about with nosy familiarity: "You've got some new barstools! What did you do with the old ones? . . . Where are the kitties? . . . Koko's on top of the fireplace, looking at us suspiciously. . . . There's Yum Yum on a barstool with her dainty paws crossed. She's adorable!"

Arch spotted the newly acquired wastebasket. "It's a Chinese water bucket! Not terribly old—probably eighteenth century." He hefted it by the carved wooden handle. "It weighs a ton!"

"That's so Yum Yum can't tip it over," Qwilleran said, "when she fishes in the wastebasket for treasures." He passed a tray with one dry sherry, one Scotch, one dubonnet, one ginger ale.

Arch was always quick with a toast. "Here's to old friends who know you well but still like you!" He helped himself to a handful from the nut bowl. "Brazil nuts! Qwill's going first-class."

"Honey, go easy on the Brazil nuts," his wife said. "They're loaded with calories!"

"That's what makes them good!"

Polly complimented Mildred on her interview with Chef Wingo.

"If he's so good," Arch asked, "why did he leave Chicago for a hick town like this?"

"Why did you come up here?" Qwilleran retorted. The two men had known each other since kindergarten in Chicago.

"Because I'm big-hearted, and you needed me to run the paper."

"You don't kid us! You wanted to get away from Down Below. You wanted to be a big frog in a small pond."

They talked about the demographic shift toward small towns . . . the Delacamp murder and the news black-out . . . Boze Campbell's gold medal for winning the caber toss . . . the proposed tri-county curling league.

Then Mildred handed Qwilleran a gift-wrapped box. "Happy whatever! Open it!"

Inside layers of tissue was a round covered box made of spalted maple.

"You mind-reader!" Qwilleran said. "I wanted to buy this, and you'd beaten me to it! How can I thank you? It's a sensational piece of woodturning. Look how precisely the cover fits! I'll keep it on the library table, near the phone."

Then Arch handed him a small flat package that could be nothing but a compact disc. "I know you like classical piano music, Qwill, and this guy is a master! Play a few tracks before we go."

Qwilleran slipped the CD into the stereo, and they listened to a little Mozart, a little Beethoven, and then Rimsky-Korsakov.

"Hey! Listen!" Qwilleran shouted. *"Flight of the Bumblebee!"*

"That should bring back memories," Arch said.

At the same time there were two thumps as Koko jumped down from the fireplace cube. He approached the stereo cautiously and sniffed the speakers.

"You know what he's looking for, don't you?" Qwilleran asked. Koko's head jerked to right and left, and he sat up on his haunches and pawed the air. When the short piece ended, he returned to his perch.

"Clever cat!" Arch said.

"Clever composer," said Qwilleran.

They drove to dinner in the Rikers' car. Mildred informed them, "There will be two menus. One is the traditional soup-and-salad-and-entree. But I suggest we all try the New Century Dining—five small courses as an adventure in tasting. Chef Wingo maintains that discriminating diners are bored with the sixteen-ounce and baked potato."

"Speak for yourself, Wingo," said Arch.

They parked in the lot behind the inn and were walking toward the carriage entrance when Qwilleran stopped abruptly and picked up something from the pavement. "A penny," he said. "A lucky penny."

"Heads or tails?" Mildred asked.

"I believe it was heads."

"That's double-luck."

"Here! You take it!"

"No! No! Finders keepers! Take it home and put it in the spalted box."

Arch said, "I wouldn't bend over for anything less than a quarter. The penny, I predict, will soon be obsolete. The smallest coin will be a nickel."

Polly said she was glad; pennies were a nuisance.

"Do you know," he went on, "that my wife is a secret penny-dropper?"

She nudged him. "You're not supposed to tell, honey."

"Tell me! I'm seriously interested," Polly insisted.

"Well . . ." Mildred began slowly, "I've had so much good luck in recent years—" She stopped and glanced at her husband. "I decided to spread it around. When I get pennies in change, I drop them here and there, one at a time, for someone else to find. In stores, on the street, at a gas pump, at the post office—anywhere. It makes me feel good to know I'm making someone else feel good."

"Charming idea!" Polly said.

"My wife's a wonderful woman," Arch said. "And I'll bet ten to one she's a better cook than this Wingo character."

In the lower lobby they were faced with a choice: to ride the elevator to the main lobby or walk up the grand staircase. Arch wanted to ride—and conserve his energy for more important things, like taking out the trash.

The main lobby was teeming with guests—many wearing tartans, most of them in town for the Scottish Gathering, several talking about the painting of Anne Mackintosh Qwilleran. The spelling of her last name was either Scottish or Danish, they said; in either case she was probably named after Lady Anne, heroine of the Scottish Rebellion in the days of Bonnie Prince Charlie.

At the entrance to the Mackintosh Room the lanky Derek Cuttlebrink towered over the maître d's desk. He seated Qwilleran's party at the best table, in front of the fabled Mackintosh crest, and presented the menu cards with a flourish. Then he whispered in Qwilleran's ear, "Gotta question to ask you—later."

Arch Riker looked suddenly pleased. "Listen! No music! No jazz! No show tunes! No electronic noise! I can eat my dinner in peace!"

His wife explained, "Chef Wingo believes in entertaining you with good food. He maintains that the voices of happy diners are the real music."

"Hear! Hear! He sounds like my kind of guy! . . . Let me look at his crazy new menu."

The wait staff consisted of young men and women from MCCC, wearing white shirts, black trousers, and plaid bowties. The one who came to Qwilleran's table delivered a well-rehearsed speech: "A traditional menu is available for those who prefer, but Chef Wingo recommends New Century Dining with its five courses: soup, appetizer, salad, savory, and dessert. Take your time and don't be afraid to order three savories and two desserts."

Qwilleran asked Mildred, "Should I know what a savory is?"

"To me, it's a little surprise—a change of flavor at the end of the meal and before the dessert."

The four of them studied the bewildering variety of options.

Arch said he would throw himself on the mercy of the chef and say, "Just bring me something good to eat."

Polly thought she could make a meal of four savories and a salad—and no dessert. She would have a toasted cheese roulade, a curried chicken liver crêpe, eggplant and avocado tartlet with cashews, and deviled crab on the half shell. Her salad would be baby spinach leaves, mandarin orange slices, and crumbled Stilton with a tomato vinaigrette dressing.

One by one they took the plunge.

First came the fun-bites, with the compliments of the chef: little somethings that he concocted on the spur of the moment—no two alike. Each guest was served a single bite-size morsel: smoked salmon sandwiched between two thin slices of strawberry and topped with a dab of sour cream and sprinkling of toasted pine nuts . . . a cherry tomato stuffed with lobster and hazelnuts . . . half a shrimp on a potato chip, crowned with a peppery tomato aspic and a miniature gaufrette of cucumber . . . an inch cube of turkey terrine smothered in black bean salsa and capers.

Comments varied: "What is it? . . . Just enjoy it and don't ask questions . . . How many more fun-bites can he invent?"

Polly asked, "How many more poems can be written? How much more music can be composed?"

Qwilleran said, "Tell that to Wingo, and you'll get free desserts for a year!"

At their table, and at surrounding tables, there was more conversation about food than about the election, the World Series, and the new car models. Chef Wingo would have approved. At one point Polly flashed her new cameo ring. Mildred found it breathtaking, and even Arch was impressed. They wanted to hear her personal reactions to the jeweler. She described the excesses of the afternoon tea: the hats, the hand-kissing, the French maids. "It's interesting," she added with a mischievous glance at Qwilleran, "for the first time in history, they had a security guard watching everyone with his hand on his gun."

Arch said wisely, "Apparently Delacamp had been tipped off that something was afoot."

There were desserts—rum cake, lemon soufflé, chocolate praline cheesecake, blackberry cobbler—and then it was over.

On the way out of the Mackintosh Room Qwilleran asked the others to wait while he had a few words with the maître d'.

"How'd you like your dinner?" Derek asked.

"It was better than Chet's Bar & Barbecue. . . . What's on your mind?"

"The police have been around, asking questions. They haven't talked to anybody in the kitchen yet, but some of the staff witnessed an incident last Tuesday and wondered if they should report it."

"What kind of incident?"

"Well, Delacamp went into the kitchen and Wingo chased him out with a skillet."

Qwilleran chuckled as he visualized the scene. "Chasing someone with a skillet or rolling pin is more symbolic than threatening. A cleaver would be something else, but . . . actually, Barry Morghan knows about the episode and explained to Delacamp that a city ordinance prohibits guests from entering the kitchen. So tell the kitchen crew they're off the hook; the manager will handle it. They don't have to snitch on their boss.

"Personally, I think Wingo has a sense of humor. The

incident has elements of slapstick comedy. Anyone who'd make a thimble-size sandwich of smoked salmon and strawberries has got to be a joker."

Qwilleran invited them back to the barn for a nightcap, and when they drove into the barnyard he jumped out of the car and unlocked the backdoor, throwing the switch that illuminated exterior and interior. What he saw was more of a surprise than strawberries and salmon; the entire kitchen was swathed in paper towels—over and around appliances, counters, and furniture. Two rolls of towels—from the kitchen sink and the snack bar—had provided fifty or sixty yards of toweling.

"You cats!" he shouted, awe mixed with annoyance.

Somewhat in shock he walked out to meet his guests. "Brace yourselves!" he told them. "The cats have prepared a little surprise for you."

Polly gasped. "Well! It's a fitting end to an unusual evening!"

Arch said, "Ye gods!"

Mildred called it conceptual art and marveled at the skill and diligence required to carry out the idea.

Koko, on the refrigerator, looked down on his masterwork. It was obviously his doing. Yum Yum was hiding somewhere, feeling guilty; she had a conscience. Koko squeezed his eyes as if accepting the compliments.

The guests, instead of having a nightcap, pitched in to unwrap the kitchen, then said goodnight. Anything else, they insisted, would be an anticlimax.

After they had gone, Qwilleran called out, "Where's

our little sweetheart?" and she came wriggling out from under the sofa. He picked her up and walked around the main floor for a while, massaging her ears and listening to her purr. And all the while he was asking himself, What was the purpose of that remarkable demonstration? Koko never did anything without a reason.

eight

SUNDAY, SEPTEMBER 13—*Better to be the head of a cat than the tail of a lion.*

Before he was fully awake, Qwilleran had a flashback to his early boyhood: walking home from first grade with his friend, Archie . . . both watching the sidewalk to avoid stepping on cracks . . . both spotting a lucky penny and grabbing for it . . . fighting about the penny until Archie's mother told them about joint ownership . . . after which they took turns carrying the penny in a pocket. In a few seconds the film of memory had faded, and he was wide awake.

Why, he asked himself, had this fragment of ancient history raced through his mind? Then he remembered the penny he had found on the parking lot and had put in his pocket simply to please Mildred. Where was it now? . . . When Qwilleran went down the ramp to start the coffeemaker, Koko was sitting on the library table— not waiting for the phone to ring but guarding the spalted maple box. Of course! That was where he had put the penny the night before. Did Koko know he was wondering about it? Was he mind-reading again?

"You rascal!" Qwilleran said. "I wish you'd learn to speak English."

Then he remembered the cat's tour de force with the paper towels. "What was that all about, young man?"

Koko scampered to the feeding station in the kitchen and waited confidently for his plate to be filled.

Later in the day Qwilleran drove to Indian Village to pick up Polly for the Scottish Gathering. In this rustic residential complex the trees were turning gold, making a striking background for the stained cedar buildings. There were fourplex apartments, a clubhouse, and clusters of condos along the Ittibittiwassee River. Four in a cluster, they were named The Birches, The Oaks, and so forth. Polly had a unit in The Willows and so did Qwilleran, although he occupied it only in winter, when the barn's cavernous spaces were hard to heat and its half-mile of driveway was blocked with snowdrifts. Indian Village might be in the country, but the county kept the roads clear, because many influential persons lived there. Another occupant of The Willows was Wetherby Goode, the WPKX meteorologist; the Cavendish sisters had recently moved to Ittibittiwassee Estates, and their unit, adjacent to Polly's, was vacant, causing her concern. The walls of the condos were thin, and noisy neighbors could be a problem.

Polly was waiting. She and Qwilleran exchanged pleasantries with the cats and then set off for the fairgrounds, both wearing their kilts, white shirts, and the Glengarry cap that had become unisex headgear.

"Lovely evening last night," she said.

"Very enjoyable."

"Any idea why Koko rampaged with the paper towels?"

"He was expressing himself."

"Carol Lanspeak called yesterday, but I didn't have a chance to tell you last night. It's about her lovely collection of French perfume bottles in the powder room. Her housekeeper has found two missing—two of the nicest. Apart from me, the only one to use the powder room was Delacamp's niece."

"I went in there to look at the collection," Qwilleran said.

"Yes, but you're not a suspect."

"Has Carol reported it?"

"No, it was too petty an incident, compared to subsequent happenings . . . And now for the good news. This morning I met my new neighbor. He's an antiquarian bookdealer from Boston!"

"You couldn't ask for a quieter neighbor."

"That's what I thought."

"Does he know he's moving to Little Antarctica?"

"He's a native of Moose County. He's returning home."

"Is he interested in winter sports? They're trying to start a curling club."

"I spoke to him only briefly, but I'm really excited about having a rare book collector next door."

Qwilleran huffed into his moustache. He too was a collector of old books, but they were not rare—just secondhand. He said, "I bought a book from Eddington's this week—something I've always wanted to read. In pretty good condition for the price. Three dollars."

"What's the title?"

"Twenty questions." It was a game they often played with book titles.

"Nineteenth century?"

"Yes."

"Fiction?"

"No."

"Male author?"

"No."

"Was she American?"

"No."

"British?"

"Yes."

"Did she also write novels?"

"Yes."

"Has any one of them been made into a film?"

"It's safe to say . . . no."

"Is the book you found . . . poetry?"

"No."

"Biography?"

"No."

"History?"

"No."

"Hmmm . . . I'm not doing very well, am I? . . . Was her work popular in her time?"

"Rephrase the question."

"Was the book you bought popular in England?"

"Yes."

"In America?"

"No."

"Ah!" Polly said with a look of discovery. "How many questions do I have left?"

"Plenty." Qwilleran could tell by her attitude that the game was lost.

"Was it a book of travel?"

"Yes."

"Is she known today for something other than her writing?"

"Yes."

"Was she the mother of a famous author?"

"Yes."

"Was his first name Anthony?"

"Yes."

"Did their last name begin with T?"

"Congratulations!" Qwilleran said. "Mrs. Trollope's *Domestic Manners of the Americans*, published in 1832."

"I've never read it," Polly admitted, "but I know she disliked Americans, their manners, their principles, and their opinions. It should be fun to read."

At the scene of the Gathering Qwilleran and Polly climbed to the top of the bleachers to ensure the best view.

First there were the marching bands, featuring bagpipes and drums and representing the counties of Lockmaster and Bixby. "The very sound of a bagpipe-and-drum band makes me teary-eyed with Scottish pride," Polly said.

Qwilleran admitted that he liked the sound but was not moved to tears. "Probably because I'm only half Scottish. I'm assuming that my father was a Dane, basing the assumption on the Qw spelling and my fondness for Danish pastry."

When the first skirling bagpipes and beating drums were heard, however, a chill ran down his spine. Eight ranks of men and women in colorful tartan garb marched in precise formations while playing *Scotland the Brave*. The spectators rose to their feet.

Then came the dancers, performing the Highland Fling and Sword Dance on portable stages while musicians bowed their fiddles in a frenzy. Young women in Highland dress bounced on the balls of their feet, their pleated kilts swirling.

Polly said, "O to be twenty years old—and weightless!"

The traditional kicks and turns and arm positions were done with micrometric exactness.

"They dance on a dime—and do it without looking!" she cried in amazement.

In the Sword Dance they bounced between the crossed blades without touching steel. When they danced in a line of three or four, their gyrations were synchronized right down to a heartbeat.

There was only one male dancer. In announcing his solo, the master of ceremonies said that Highland dancing was originally an athletic challenge for men, requiring both skill and endurance.

Qwilleran said to Polly, "Do you know the bozo who won the gold medal for the caber toss?"

"I'm afraid not. I know several John Campbells, but none could toss anything heavier than a horseshoe."

The final event was the pibroch, performed by the police chief of Pickax. The centuries-old tradition called for a lone piper to play a succession of pieces increasing in difficulty, all the while walking slowly about the stage. For the piper it was a challenge; for the audience it was a mesmerizing experience, almost spiritual in its effect. The crowd watched in total silence. Polly claimed to have been in a trance.

Qwilleran said, "In the Scottish community Andy is considered the master of the pibroch." And he thought, I'll invite him to the barn for a drink tonight.

They were walking back to the brown van in the parking lot when Qwilleran swooped down on a penny and dropped it in his pocket. Polly had not noticed.

On the way home she asked, "What are you writing for your Tuesday column?"

"Glad you asked. Thanks to our conversation on fibs, I'm planning a dissertation on prevarications of all kinds: untruths, falsehoods, canards, whoppers, taradiddles, fibble-fabble, and just plain bull. I'm asking, What is the difference between a little white lie and big dirty one? . . . What are the dangers of lying to your boss, your spouse, a court judge, the Internal Revenue Service? . . . What was the most heinous lie in Shakespeare?"

"In *Othello*," she replied without hesitation. "Iago maliciously lies about Desdemona's handkerchief, and it leads to her murder."

"Good! Go to the head of the class. And how about Mark Twain? Did he have anything to say about lies?"

"He had something to say about everything!" She reflected briefly. "He said the difference . . . between a cat and a lie was that . . . a cat has only nine lives."

That brought up the subject of the Mark Twain Festival. According to old letters and diaries found in Moose County, the author had lectured in Pickax in 1895 while touring the northern states, and he had captivated the audience with his wit and forthright opinions. There was no documented evidence that he had slept at the Pickax hotel; on the other hand, there was no proof that he had not! And the Mackintosh Inn had decided to rename the presidential suite *The Mark Twain Suite*. Already his portrait hung above the bed where Delacamp had been murdered.

Qwilleran told Polly, "The murder in the presidential suite has caused the festival promoters to postpone it until October."

"Is that a good month?" she asked. "It could be cold."

"There's a meeting Wednesday to discuss the pros and cons."

Qwilleran dropped Polly at her condo for her Sunday ritual of getting herself together for the workweek. What it entailed he had no idea, and he would never ask. He himself went home to feed the cats and talk to them: "You guys missed a good show this weekend. Next year we'll have a Feline Gathering. Koko can toss the caber, and Yum Yum can dance the Highland Fling on the balls of her paws."

Whether he talked nonsense or recited the Declaration of Independence, their reaction was the same: purring, looking wide-eyed, and twitching their tails. As he discovered, Koko had done a little caber-tossing of his own;

the floor of the library area was littered with the fat yellow pencils that Qwilleran kept in his ceramic pencil-holder.

There were fang-marks in the soft wood. "That cat!" he said aloud as he gathered them off the rug. "One day it's paper towels; the next day it's pencils!"

"Yargle!" came a response from the kitchen, as Koko tried to yowl and swallow at the same time.

For his own Sunday night supper Qwilleran went to Rennie's at the inn. It was quiet. Weekend guests had checked out, and the week's business travelers had not yet registered. After having a Reuben sandwich, he stopped at the reception desk to chat with Lenny Inchpot.

"How'd you like the games?" the clerk asked. "My mom saw you there with Mr. MacWhannell and said you two had the best-looking knees at the whole Gathering."

"That sounds just like your mother!"

"How'd you like Boze's caber toss?"

"Fantastic."

"When he went to the podium to get the gold medal hung around his neck, I was so proud, I could bust! It's not real gold, but it's a shot in the arm for a guy with no real ambition—except to win the state lottery. One day he asked me, 'How much is a million dollars?' Boze isn't smart, but he's big, and it doesn't hurt to have a muscle-man behind the desk after midnight. Another time he asked me why the days were getting shorter. It keeps me on my toes, sort of."

"How do you answer his questions?"

"Usually I give him a straight answer, best I can, but the other day I went for the joke. He asked me, 'Where's Brazil?' I remembered that line from *Charley's Aunt* and said, 'Where the nuts come from.' It fell flat, of course, so I told him Brazil's in South America, which is south of North America, and I ended up drawing a map of the western hemisphere on the back of an envelope. See what I mean?"

"What's his chief interest?"

"Eating. Never gets enough food! My mom would be willing to teach him to cook for a living, but . . ."

A business traveler came to the desk asking for a studio room with computer desk, and Qwilleran moved away until the transaction was complete. Then he asked Lenny, "Has the homicide had any effect on business?"

"It doesn't seem to bother the guests. In fact, some of them find it kind of exciting. But the staff talks about it a lot, among themselves. Yesterday the day porter saw a locksmith truck from Bixby pull up to the back door. The police took him upstairs. In half an hour he left."

"Boze must have been on duty at the time of the crime."

"Yeah, and he told me what he told the police. Around two or two-thirty the lobby was quiet, and he heard the elevator go from the ground floor to one of the upper floors. He thought some guest was coming in when the bars closed. A little later he heard the elevator go down again, as if somebody had just come in for a nightcap or something."

"Or something," Qwilleran said. "Well, good to talk with you, Lenny. Keep up the good work!" He glanced at the carpet, picked something up, and dropped it in his pocket. With amusement he remembered what Iris Cobb used to say: "A whirligig is just a whirligig, but two whirligigs are a pair, and three are a collection."

He was now a collector. It was surprising how many pennies dropped through people's fingers or through holes in their pockets. Or were they purposely dropped by penny-droppers like Mildred?

At the barn he put the newfound pennies into the spalted maple box and checked his messages on the answering machine. He immediately returned Larry Lanspeak's call.

"Qwill! I've been trying to reach you all day!"

"When did you get in from—wherever you were?"

"This morning. Carol had phoned my hotel on Friday, and I couldn't believe the news! But I met a Chicago buyer at the merchandising show, and he told me something quite interesting about Delacamp. That wasn't always his name. His last name was Campau. That's spelled C-A-M-P-A-U, and he was in partnership with a French gemologist whose name was spelled F-E-Y-D-E-A-U. But it seems that Americans had a problem pronouncing the firm's name and even remembering it. So Campau became Delacamp, and F-E-Y-D-E-A-U became F-I-D-O . . . Do you follow me?"

"Woof woof!"

"Okay, wise guy! Get off the line."

"I'll be on my best behavior. Tell me the rest of the story."

Larry went on. "Fido accused Delacamp of embezzling money from the firm and took him to court, but he lost his case for lack of proof. There had been a lot of nasty publicity, however, so Delacamp sued Fido for libel—and won a sizable judgment! How do you like that?"

"Interesting bit of intrigue!"

"That's what I thought. I've always been curious about Delacamp's cash transactions . . . Don't forget: the genealogy club meets Wednesday night, and you're invited."

It was late evening—the hour when Qwilleran had often phoned Andrew Brodie at home. The chief answered brusquely.

"It's a long time between drinks, Andy, and I happen to have some double-malt."

"Be right there." A few minutes later he tramped into the barn, looking grouchy.

Qwilleran said with enthusiasm, "Andy, I saw the pibroch for the first time today, and I want to tell you it's a transcendental experience!"

"Whatever that means."

"You were superb! Polly was with me, and she said your performance put her under a spell."

Brodie grunted. He was not accustomed to compliments.

"Was your wife there?"

"Nah. She's seen it a hundred times."

"How about your grandchildren?"

"Nah. They're not into that stuff."

"It must give you satisfaction to play music that gives people deep feelings."

"Nah. It's just something I do." Brodie flung the suggestion away with an impatient gesture.

"Who was the man with a video recorder?"

"Some fella from the Scottish Museum in Lockmaster. Thinks they can sell 'em. But it won't work with the pibroch. There has to be a direct connection between the piper and the listener."

"Exactly what I was trying to say," Qwilleran told him. "Take a seat and pour yourself a drink."

His guest dropped into one of the new barstools. "Nice stool!" He glanced around the barn. "Where's your smart cat?"

"On top of the fireplace, watching you. Don't make a false move."

There was a *thump* as Koko jumped down to the surface of the library table, making the visitor wince instinctively, but Koko merely began dragging yellow pencils from the pencil holder.

Qwilleran explained, "He likes to sink his fangs in the soft wood of a pencil. I did the same thing when I was a kid, learning to write. I chewed every pencil. Arch Riker, my seatmate, wrote with his left ear down on the desk and his right hand moving the pencil four inches from his nose. The teacher thought we were a couple of weirdos."

Brodie chuckled. "It seems to me you turned out all right. Both of you! The worst I ever did was to try lickin' frozen railway tracks. Almost lost a tongue."

"Lucky you didn't lose an entire head!" Qwilleran pushed the nut bowl toward him. "Try these. Absolutely fresh!"

"What are the big ones? They're big as horse chestnuts!"

"Brazil nuts. We never had them up here until the Sip 'n' Nibble Shop opened. Good, aren't they? . . . I didn't see you at the games yesterday."

"Had to take my wife shopping."

"When Boze Campbell tossed a perfect caber, three out of three, it was a historic moment in Moose County. It'll be all over the paper tomorrow. He's a desk clerk at the inn, you know."

"I know. He was on duty at the time of the homicide, and all he noticed was the elevator going up and down. He's a good athlete but not smart. What can you expect? He was born with two strikes against him."

"He was an orphan, I hear."

"A foundling!" said Brodie. "And I'm the one that found him!"

"Is that so?"

"Yep. Twenty-five years ago when I was working for the sheriff. There was an old shack on Chipmunk Road that we had orders to keep an eye on. Kids used to hang out there. One night before Halloween I was on patrol and stopped to check it out. It was a fire hazard, what with oil lamps, candles, and smokin'. I saw no cars parked, no lights inside, but I heard a baby cryin'. I knew it wasn't some kind of bird or animal. I went in with my flashlight, and there on an old broken-down table was a soup carton with this little red thing no bigger'n a skinned squirrel, and it was yellin' its head off! There was no note—no clue—nothin'! I rushed it to old Dr. Goodwinter's house—remember him?—and got him out of bed. The mother was never identified."

"How did he get named John Campbell? That's a prominent name around here."

"Social Services took over, and at first he was just John Doe, but nobody wanted to adopt him and give him a name, so they took the one off the soup carton." Brodie

water. "It would help," the chief said, "if Old Gumshoe here would tell us something we don't know already."

"Such as?" Qwilleran asked lightly.

"Who's the girl? She registered at the inn as Pamela North. An alias, of course. She probably has several, now that IDs are a dime a dozen." He lowered his voice. "This is strictly off the record, of course, but the SBI has found a pattern in her MO."

"You speak as if she's the brain of the operation, and yet she was meek as milk when I met her at the dinner party."

"Did your smart cat meet her?"

"No, he never had the pleasure, but I'll tell you one thing he did, Andy: He howled in the middle of the night at the precise time of Delacamp's death."

Brodie grunted. "Dogs do that."

"But only when it's someone they know. I'll show you something else dogs don't do. I'm going to play a piano recording of *Flight of the Bumblebee*. Watch Koko!"

He slipped the disc into the stereo, setting it for track three. The pianist's fingers started to fly. From his lofty perch Koko looked down on the men and the machine. They waited. The cat did nothing.

"I don't get it!" Brodie said. "What's he doing?"

"He's making a fool of me—that's what he's doing. It's his favorite hobby."

nine

Monday, September 14—*A cat in gloves catches no mice.*

While brushing the cats' coats that morning, Qwilleran kept up a running patter to relax them. He said, "Culvert's calendar tells us it's Monday, but what do you care? All days are alike to you guys. No Saturday night dates. No Monday blues. No Tuesday deadlines." After the grooming they liked a reading session, and he chose Mark Twain's story about the jumping frog. Koko wanted *Oedipus Rex* but Qwilleran said it was too tragic for their tender ears.

His own day started with a visit to the public library, where he was greeted warmly by Mac and Katie, the feline mascots. They knew he always brought a pocketful of crunchy treats. On the mezzanine he found Polly in her glass-enclosed office, eating her lunch—a tuna sandwich and carrot sticks. "Good news!" she said. "Our bookmobile will be back in circulation by the end of the week!"

The vehicle had been acquired through private donations and a matching grant from the K Fund. Manufactured by a maker of school buses, it looked like a school bus without windows. The interior had bookshelves instead of seats, and hundreds of books could be circulated to communities that were without libraries. Unfortunately, it was painted white, giving rise to a public outcry. Letters to the newspaper said it looked like a milk truck, an ambulance, a laundry van. To settle the unrest, readers were invited to suggest ideas. The best was selected by a panel of civic leaders, Polly included, and the bus was sent to a commercial art studio in Lockmaster to be repainted. The panel's selection was top secret. And now it was returning to Pickax, shrouded in a tarpaulin until the Thursday unveiling.

Qwilleran said to Polly, "How about telling me, off the record, what the new design is."

"My lips are sealed," she said smugly.

"Could I sneak a peek under the tarp? Or do you have armed guards?"

"You declined an invitation to serve on the panel, so you'll have to wait, along with the other citizens. . . . Have some carrot sticks."

"No thanks."

"They're good for you."

"I know. That's why I don't want any."

Qwilleran's next stop was the newspaper office, where he handed in his copy to Junior Goodwinter, the young managing editor.

"Is something wrong?" asked the editor. "You're a day

early!" Usually the "Qwill Pen" met its deadline with only minutes to spare. Then Junior said, "Wait till you see today's edition! On page one the Highland Games are the banner story, with some great shots of the caber cavorting in midair and Campbell getting his gold medal—plus a sidebar on Brodie and the pibroch. On the picture page we have the dancers, fiddlers, pipe-and-drum bands, and a candid of a couple of stalwart Scots in kilts, eating bridies. On page two we congratulate Homer Tibbitt on his ninety-eighth birthday. And on the editorial page we have some interesting letters to the editor."

"Interesting-good? Or interesting-bad?"

"Wait and see."

"By the way, Junior, do you know anything about an old shack on Chipmunk Road near the Big B minesite? It's said to be a hangout for kids."

"Oh, that! It was torn down during the roadside beautification campaign, but there was so much public sentiment attached to it, the county salvaged the boards and auctioned them off. There are plenty of stories about that dump."

"Do you have time for lunch? I'll treat at Rennie's."

"Can't. Arch has called an emergency meeting during the lunch hour."

"What happened?" Qwilleran asked. "Did the water cooler spring a leak? Did somebody cancel a subscription?"

"*Goodbye!*" Junior barked. "And I'll see that they misspell your name in tomorrow's paper."

Fellow staffers always teased Qwilleran about his personal crusade against typographical errors, and on one occasion they conspired to sprinkle his entire column

with typos. Even he had to chuckle over the comic enor-
mity of the April Fool trick.

Now it was Monday, September 14, and he liked to
lunch with someone on the first day of the workweek.
On the way out of the building he came face to face with
a wiry, vigorous man in farmer's denims and feed cap—
Sig Dutcher, the county's agricultural agent. They met
often at the Dimsdale Diner, where farmers gathered for
coffee, agritalk, gossip, and a few laughs.

Qwilleran said, "Sig, you mud-devil! What brings you
in from the back forty?"

"Just delivering some red-hot ag news to your business
editor."

"Are you free for lunch at the Mackintosh Inn? My
treat."

"Sure. Can I go like this?"

"Of course. We'll have a burger in the coffee shop."

It was the agent's first visit to the refurbished inn, and
he was thunderstruck. When he saw Rennie's with its
clean white walls and bright blue and green tables, he
said, "It beats the Dimsdale Diner!"

"Anything new at the Diner?" Qwilleran asked after
they took seats in the high-backed chairs. "I haven't
been there for a while."

"Well . . . Benny broke his leg in a tractor rollover . . .
Calvin had a couple of cows die on him . . . Doug's
daughter won a blue ribbon at the fair for a black-face
ewe . . . Spencer's wife needs an operation, and their insurance lapsed . . . That's about it . . . How about you,
Qwill? Are you still eating a McIntosh a day to keep the
doctor away?"

"Actually, I have nothing against the medical profession, but I do like apples, and my favorite happens to be the McIntosh, if I can't get Winesaps."

"We don't get many Winesaps around here, but we have one of the best McIntosh orchards in the state. And thereby hangs a tale that might steal its way into your column. Did you know there were no so-called eating apples on this continent before the European settlers brought them? Only crab apples. And here's another interesting fact: The millions of McIntosh trees in the U.S. are all direct descendents of a single seedling found in the Canadian wilderness."

"How did it get there?" Qwilleran asked.

"That's the mystery! In 1832 a farmer in Ontario was clearing land when he found this seedling. He transplanted it to his farmyard, and it bore fruit for thirty years. Then his son found out about grafting fruit trees, and the rest is history."

"It sounds like a 'Qwill Pen' story, all right."

"That's what I thought, Qwill. If you go to my office in the county building and ask for the McIntosh file, they'll copy a lot of material for you."

While waiting for their burgers they discussed the Highland Games, Bixby's proposal to build a gambling casino, the remarkable Border collie, and the weather.

"Any new jokes at the Diner?" Qwilleran asked.

"Did you hear the one about the two bulls in the—"

He was interrupted by the waitperson's announcement, "You didn't say if you wanted fries, so I brought you some anyway. What else can I get for you . . . gentlemen?"

Dutcher asked for red pepper sauce; Qwilleran wanted horseradish.

"Did you hear that?" the agent asked. "She called us gentlemen!"

"They've been instructed not to refer to customers as 'you guys' any more. How do you react to being called a gentleman?"

"It comes as a shock. Maybe it'll help me keep my elbows off the table. My wife will approve."

"How's the family?"

"All fine, thank you. The boy's going out for football. The girl enrolled at MCCC. She's decided she wants to be a large-animal vet, which is funny because she's such a little thing. . . . But let me tell you the latest! Becky's working part-time as housekeeper's aide at the inn, and she's the one who found the body Friday morning!"

"That must have been a jolt for a college freshman."

"You're right! It doesn't happen every day! . . . You see, her instructions were to make up the 301 suite and 301A every morning between seven-thirty and eight-thirty, while the occupants were downstairs at breakfast. As usual she knocked before using her passkey, but the door was chained! She went to the other room and got right in! . . . We're not supposed to talk about this, Qwill, but I know it won't go any further."

"Don't worry."

"First thing, she noticed the assistant's bed hadn't been slept in. She opened the connecting door, and there he was—lying in bed with a pillow over his head! She backed out, reported to the housekeeper, told the police everything they wanted to know, and kept her cool. But then she went to pieces and had to be driven home."

"Good for Becky! She performed like a Trojan."

"Who do you think did it, Qwill?"

"I believe all the suspicion points to someone from Down Below."

"Yeah," said the agent. "That's the consensus at the Diner."

Before leaving the inn, Qwilleran bought a newspaper in the lobby and sat in the Stickley alcove to peruse it. Alternately he approved of the coverage and huffed into his moustache with adverse reactions. He approved generally of the handling of the Scottish Gathering and Homer Tibbitt's ninety-eighth birthday, but did they have to continue using a thirty-year-old photo of the old gentleman? And were they overdoing the praise heaped on the gold medal winner? Boze was a naive young man, and it could go to his head. And did they have to use that photo of "two unidentified Scots eating bridies"? Everyone in the county knew the faces of Qwilleran and MacWhannell; it was all too coy. They should have given more space to Andrew Brodie and the pibroch. And why was the lone male dancer overlooked? Even the editorial was too soppy in Qwilleran's opinion—about the youth who lacked family advantages but had persevered to finish school, hone his athletic skills, enroll in college, and take a responsible part-time job. . . . Still. It was not a columnist's privilege to edit the paper. Qwilleran went on to read the letters to the editor:

To the Editor—Come November, another election . . . with voters staying home as usual. Do you

know why? Because they're used to being served refreshments in public places: at meetings and ex-
hibits, in banks and stores, at church and funerals.
To get a good turnout on Election day, just advertise: "Vote Tuesday—Refreshments Served." All
you need are a few cookies and some weak punch.
—Herbert Watts.

To the Editor—Bixby County wants to build a
"gaming" casino to bolster its economy and create
jobs. Is that a euphemism for "gambling" or is it true
that Bixbyites can't spell? Whatever, they plan to
build it half a block from the county line. Since
gambling establishments are prohibited in Moose
County, our good folk will beat a path to the "gaming" casino, and it will be Moose County money
that bolsters the Bixby economy. Smart thinking,
guys!—Mitch Campbell.

To the Editor—I am a woman 40 years old. I
have just learned to read and write. It gives me a
wonderful feeling. I hope I will get better jobs now.
I always tried to hide my secret. I was afraid to get
married because my husband would find out. I want
to thank my tutor for being so kind and helpful.
(Name withheld.)

Qwilleran's last scheduled stop for Monday was Ittibittiwassee Estates, where he would pay his annual birthday
visit to the county's most prominent nonagenarian. The
development was nowhere near the picturesque river
after which it was named. It occupied a ridge between

Chipmunk Road and Bloody Creek, neither of which would make an appealing name for a retirement community. The main building was a large four-story structure with a steeply pitched roof that gave the impression of a resort hotel in Switzerland or the Rockies.

Homer Tibbitt and his wife, Rhoda, had moved there in order to have assisted care, when and if necessary. Qwilleran found them on the top floor. Rhoda—a sweet-faced, white-haired octogenarian with a hearing aid—greeted him warmly. "It wouldn't be a birthday without a visit from you, Qwill. Homer is waiting for you in his lair."

A sneeze came from an adjoining room. "Come into my library," came a reedy, high-pitched voice, "if you're not allergic to dust!" Scrawny and angular, Homer sat like a potentate in a pile of soft pillows cushioning his bony frame. His face had the furrows and wrinkles of his age, but his spirit was still lively. Now official historian for Moose County, he had been a high school principal—and a lifelong bachelor—when he retired. Not too long ago he had married a retired teacher ten years his junior.

"He married me because I still had a driver's license," she said sweetly.

"She married me because she thought I had a future," said Homer. "She was a wild thing at eighty-two. I tamed her."

"Shall we have tea?" she asked with her gentle smile.

When she left the room, Qwilleran set up his tape recorder on the tea table. "Well, Homer, do you have any profound thoughts to share on the occasion of your natal day? Anything fit to print?"

The old man cleared his throat at great length before saying, "Glad you asked. It so happens I came upon my childhood bankbook a few days ago, and it loosed a flood of memories. I was born in the town of Little Hope, but I had the grand hope of becoming rich and having my own horse and saddle. My father could afford to give me spending money—ten cents a week—and I always took a penny to the general store and bought a week's supply of candy. The rest went into my cast-iron bank. It was like an apple, with a cork in the bottom, which I removed twice a week in order to count my growing fortune. When I had amassed fifty pennies, I deposited them in my bank account. The teller would write the total in the right-hand column—so I could always see my net worth at a glance. Sometimes the bank added a few pennies interest. I was always amazed and overjoyed to get something for nothing."

"Did you ever save up enough to buy your horse?" Qwilleran asked.

"No, but I bought a two-wheeled bike—a dollar down and a dollar a month. I couldn't believe it when they said I could take it home and ride it before it was paid for! It seemed like incredible largesse on the part of the general store."

Rhoda had poured the tea and handed him a cup, saying, "Stop talking and drink it while it's hot."

"She's a tyrant about hot tea! Wants me to scald my gums!"

She murmured to Qwilleran, "He forgets to drink it and then complains because it's cold. I didn't know about his quaint foibles when I married him."

"Bosh! You knew everything! You'd been chasing me for years!"

"You didn't run very fast, dear."

Qwilleran interrupted the comedy routine that the happy couple repeated on every visit. "I suppose there was no income tax in those days."

"Not until I had my first teaching assignment. It was in a one-room schoolhouse with a pot-bellied stove. I didn't earn much money, and at the end of the year the government took four dollars away from me. For income tax, they said. I thought I'd been robbed! Now all you hear from Washington is: seventy million . . . twelve billion . . . six trillion! Sounds like the old Kingfish character on the radio. You don't remember him. You're too young."

Qwilleran said, "Homer, you should start writing your autobiography."

"There's plenty of time for that," the old man said testily. "I intend to live until that villain in the mayor's office is thrown out on his ear!"

"Then you'll live forever, dear," said Rhoda, explaining to Qwilleran, "Mr. Blythe is automatically reelected every term because his mother was a Goodwinter." Between sips of tea she was snipping a scrap of black paper with tiny scissors.

"May I ask what you're doing?" Qwilleran asked.

"Cutting a silhouette of you. My grandmother taught me how. It was a popular art in Victorian days. She had a silhouette signed by Edouarte that would be quite valuable today, and she promised to leave it to me, but my cousin in Ohio got it."

"Rhoda and her rascally relatives!" Homer complained. "They're driving me to an early grave!"

Qwilleran said, "I have no relatives at all, and I'd gladly settle for a couple of rascals."

"Take some of Rhoda's, Qwill! Take her two cousins in Ohio."

She said, "But . . . the Aunt Fanny you inherited from . . ."

"She was my mother's best friend—not my real aunt."

"And how is dear Polly? I haven't seen her since we moved out here. I used to drive Homer to the library every day, and I always had a little chat with Polly."

"Do you find it stimulating enough—living out here?"

"Oh, yes! We have book clubs and discussion groups and lectures. Last week we had a speaker from the Literacy Council. Do you know it's easier to teach adults how to read than to teach children? Adults have developed certain skills and talents and are more realistic."

Homer was showing sings of drowsiness, and Qwilleran thought it was time to leave. Rhoda gave him his silhouette in an envelope, saying, "Put this in a little frame and give it to Polly. She'll want to put it on her desk at the library. Your head has very good lines."

As soon as he reached the parking lot he opened the envelope. The silhouette was hardly larger than a postage stamp, yet it was a recognizable likeness. The moustache protruded more than he thought it should. Perhaps it needed trimming. The head was a little flat on top, but generally he agreed that the lines of his head were good. On the way home he stopped at Lanspeak's and bought a small frame in the gift shop.

. . .

In the the early evening, as Qwilleran was preparing the cats' dinner, Koko muttered a small growl and jumped to the counter to peer out the window. In a minute or two a small red car came out of the woods—Celia Robinson's car. Yet he always welcomed her with anticipation, not growls.

Going out to meet the vehicle, Qwilleran saw a strange woman at the wheel. She rolled the driver's window down and said, "Mr. Qwilleran? Celia Robinson wanted me to deliver some things. She's very busy." She handed over the three cartons that were on the passenger seat.

"That was thoughtful of her. Are you her new assistant?"

"Yes sir." He summed her up as healthy-looking but plain, with glasses and with hair drawn tightly back.

"And what is your name?" he asked pleasantly.

"Nora, sir."

"Thank you, Nora . . . Follow the driveway around the big tree, and you'll be headed back to Main Street."

"Yes, sir. Thank you, sir."

As soon as the cartons were in the refrigerator Qwilleran phoned Celia and told her how much he appreciated the food delivery.

"I'm working on a big luncheon for tomorrow and thought you wouldn't mind if I sent Nora. What did you think of her?"

"What can I say? She seems to be neat and clean and polite."

"Yes, she has nice manners," Celia said. "She worked for the Sprenkles for years as a housemaid and also helped the cook. She's the student I tutored."

"Is she the one whose letter ran in today's paper?"

"Did they print it? She'll be thrilled!"

"Did you help her with it, Celia?"

"Only with punctuation—and the spelling of a couple of words. Did you open the cartons? The tuna salad is for sandwiches. The bread pudding is laced with chocolate sauce. And I made you a lovely ham loaf."

"What's the difference between a lovely ham loaf and an unlovely one?"

Her shrill laugh pierced his left ear, and he scowled at the receiver.

"Go back to your chicken à la king," he said.

When she went back to her kitchen and he went to stock the refrigerator, his mind was not on ham loaf or bread pudding. He was thinking, How did that cat know it was not Celia driving Celia's car?

ten

Tuesday, September 15—*A carriage without a horse goes nowhere.*

For the morning reading session Koko selected *Oedipus Rex* again, and his choice was vetoed for the third time. Qwilleran thought, It's more than fish glue in the old binding that attracts him. There might be a hundred-dollar bill leafed between the pages, or a love letter, or the deed to a gold mine. (A brief Gold Rush had been part of Moose County's history.) Riffling through the pages he found nothing—not even a coffee stain or smear of chocolate, confirming his guess that the book had never been read. So the Sophocles volume went back on the shelf, and Qwilleran read from Mark Twain's autobiography—the part about the two tomcats fighting on the roof.

Later he went downtown to buy supplies for the evening's cocktail party. He was inviting Barry Morghan to meet some of the town's movers and shakers. Barry had met Polly on Labor Day. Now he would meet Hixie Rice, promotion director for the *Something;* Dwight Somers, local public relations counsel; and Maggie Sprenkle, who had connections with all the old moneyed families. After cocktails the guests would be taken to dinner at the Old Stone Mill—the best restaurant in the county until the Mackintosh Room opened.

At the Sip 'n' Nibble Shop Qwilleran purchased champagne (the best label) and mixed nuts (the luxury blend, with plenty of pecans and Brazil nuts). Thoughtfully he bought half a pound of almonds for Polly and anyone else on a diet. Jack Nibble and Joe Sipp were both in the store, talkative as usual. Longtime partners, they had the habit of completing each other's thoughts. They said:

"Didn't know Pickax could be so exciting!"

"New hotel, gold medal winner, and murder—"

"All in one week."

"The guy they killed came in here once—"

"Looking to buy rum—"

"Ticked off because we handle only wine."

"Bought some luxury mix, though."

"His assistant, or whatever, tagged along after him, demurely."

"His kind likes that kind."

While Qwilleran was downtown, Pat O'Dell's janitorial service gave the barn what they called a fluff-up: quick tidying, superficial dusting, and vaccuuming here and there.

To stay out of their way, Qwilleran killed an hour at Lois's Luncheonette, having a slice of apple pie and reading the Tuesday *Something.* Lenny, he expected, would barge in after classes, howling for coffee and pie. Instead, the young man slouched into the lunchroom and went directly to the kitchen for quiet words with his mother. When he emerged with a plate and a mug, Qwilleran hailed him. "Anything wrong, Lenny?"

"Boze didn't show up for work last night," he replied in a low voice as he slid into the booth. "He had Saturday and Sunday nights off but was supposed to relieve me last night at midnight. No show! No excuse! No nothing! I called his rooming house, but the phone was on the answering machine until six A.M." Lenny took a gulp of coffee.

"What happens in a situation like that?"

"I notified the resident manager, and she covered for him. But I was really burned, Qwill! I drove around to all the bars until two o'clock, looking for his truck. No luck. He cut his classes this morning, too."

Qwilleran said, "That was a lot of glory for a neophyte. I admit I wondered how he'd react."

Lenny wasn't listening. "Did he go on a colossal binge in Bixby? Did he get in a fight down there? Did they drug his beer? Did he fall in with some groupies?"

"How do you think Morghan will feel about it? It's only one night that he goofed off. Saturday and Sunday were—"

"Mr. Morghan is a decent boss, but rules are rules."

"It could be a traffic accident. Did anyone check the police and the hospitals?"

"The resident said she would. There'd be a radio news bulletin if anything bad happened to a gold medalist. I think Boze is AWOL, and it reflects on me. I'm the one who recommended him for the job. Other people thought I was crazy. . . . You know, Mr. Q, sometimes I think I'm jinxed. I try hard, but something always happens. First, the hotel gets bombed by some psycho, and I lose the only girl I was ever serious about. Also, my job is bombed out for a year. The interim job you got for me turned sour when I was framed. . . . See what I mean?"

Qwilleran said, "If Boze doesn't report tonight, you should file a Missing Person report, and the police will put a tri-county check on his truck." He stood up to leave. "And don't let me hear any defeatist talk from you! Nothing can get you down, Lenny. You're like Lois!"

Polly, first to arrive at the barn that evening, said, "Maggie will be the only native in the party tonight."

"That's all right," Qwilleran replied. "It'll show Barry how outsiders adjust to small-town living without losing their identity."

"Is there anything I can do?"

"You might look at the photo-prints of the Gathering on the coffee table and take whatever you want. I ordered extras."

The dinner guests arrived at the barn in separate vehicles, making the barnyard look like a used-car lot.

Polly had brought a large book from the library, featuring old photos of Moose County: mines, lumber camps, shipyards, sawmills, rooming houses, log cabins, logging wagons. She told Barry Morghan, "You might like to take it home and browse through it, then drop it in the drive-through bookbox behind the library."

"Great!" the innkeeper said.

Then Maggie presented him with a framed photo of a grim stone building with a painted sign: HOTEL. She said, "This was the original Pickax Hotel and staff. You might like to hang it in your office."

On the front steps were the manager, in sidewhiskers and frock coat; the hotel's carriage driver, with top hat and whip; and long-skirted, white-capped chambermaids and cooks. All were solemn-faced. The only happy touch was a stray dog of mixed breed, sitting on the sidewalk and enjoying the excitement.

"Great!" Barry said. "I'll have a companion photo taken—the Mackintosh Inn and its smiling staff."

"And a dog," Hixie suggested.

Maggie said, "The animal shelter has one exactly like the original. They'll let you borrow him for the photo."

"The *Something* will run before-and-after shots on the picture page," Qwilleran promised.

Then Hixie presented Barry with a small gift-wrapped box. "This is a memento of something that never happened—Moose County's First and Probably Last Ice Festival."

He opened it and found a three-inch lapel button with a polar bear motif.

She said, "It's one of only fifteen thousand that we were stuck with."

"Great!"

"In fifty or seventy-five years it should be worth something. Hang onto it."

"I will! I will!" Barry said as he pinned it on his blazer. There was an obvious moment of appreciative rapport between the two, and the others started talking all at once:

"There were some interesting letters to the editor yesterday."

"How's the Mark Twain Festival coming along? Does anyone know?"

"I saw Homer Tibbitt yesterday. He's as spirited as ever."

"Where are the cats?" Maggie asked.

"Yes, where are they?" Polly wanted to know.

"They've scrutinized all of you and found you harmless," Qwilleran replied. "They're sleeping on top of the refrigerator."

"Would anyone like to see Amanda's campaign poster?" Dwight asked.

"Yes! Yes!"

"Who's Amanda?" Barry asked.

Everyone explained at once: "She's Fran Brodie's boss, owner of the design studio . . . She's going to run for mayor . . . She hates the incumbent! . . . She's been on the city council for ages! . . . She's a little odd, but everyone likes her oddities."

"What kind of oddities?" Barry asked. "Name two."

"She's a successful businesswoman but looks like a scarecrow."

"She speaks her mind and doesn't care where the chips fall."

"And what about the incumbent? I met him at the opening reception, and he seemed quite . . . smooth."

"Smooth like a snake," said Maggie. "He was the high school principal until a scandal involving girl students. Then he became an investment counselor and ran for mayor. He was elected because his mother was a Goodwinter. He keeps getting reelected for the same reason—not because he's ever done the city any good."

Dwight had opened his portfolio and produced a poster with a photo of a handsome man and the message: VOTE FOR BLYTHE. He said, "This is the poster that gets him elected every time. Now I'll show you the poster that will beat him in November."

It was a caricature of a woman with unruly hair, slightly crossed eyes, and a downturned mouth, and the message was: WE'D RATHER HAVE AMANDA.

Polly said, "Everyone knows who she is. She's a *real* Goodwinter!"

Barry said, "I'll vote for her! Where do I register?"

When Qwilleran went to the refrigerator for another bottle of champagne, Barry followed him and said in a low voice, "Our hero didn't show up for work last night—and no explanation."

"So I heard. What happens now?"

"Two cuts and he's suspended. After a week he's fired, even if he is a celebrity. You can't run a hotel that way."

Back in the lounge area, after the cork was popped, Barry asked, "What was the hotel like before it was bombed?"

Everyone groaned. "Dismal! . . . Depressing! . . . But clean!"

Then Dwight told his towel rod story. "When I came to Pickax, I stayed at the hotel a couple of weeks. The bed was okay; the plumbing worked; but the towel rod kept falling off the wall. Every day I reported it, and every day it was fixed. But whenever I took a towel, it clattered to the floor again. Once it crashed in the middle of the night for no reason at all. After I left, the hotel was bombed. Windows blew out. Chandeliers fell. But Fran Brodie reported that the towel rod in 209 was still on the wall!"

"Great story!" said Barry. "We'll give you a weekend in the new 209 without charge."

The restaurant called The Old Stone Mill had been a working grist mill on a rushing stream in pioneer days—with a waterwheel that turned and groaned and creaked. Now the stream had run dry and the wheel was a reproduction, electrically powered. But the original stone walls and ponderous timbers gave the mill a romantic atmosphere for dining. Qwilleran's party had a round table for six, and Barry managed to sit next to Hixie and get better acquainted.

Dwight interrupted their tête-à-tête with a question. "What do you think about Moose County, Barry?"

"It's great! Absolutely great!"

"Do you have any questions to ask Qwill's panel of Pickax pundits?"

"Yes! My brother and his wife are planning to move up here and wondering where to live. Any suggestions?"

"If they want a roomy old-fashioned house, Pleasant Street has some beauties, and they're within walking distance of everything. If they're interested in an apartment or condo, I recommend Indian Village. It's in a wooded area, a short drive from town. I live there."

"I live there," said Hixie.

"I live there," Polly chimed in, "and so does Qwill in

the winter. There are walking paths along the river and a clubhouse."

"Sounds great!" Barry said. "My sister-in-law is an artist, and she asked about the art climate around here."

Qwilleran answered that question. "We have a new art center for exhibitions, classes, workshops, and lectures. What is her special interest?"

"Batik."

Polly said, "No one in this area does batik. Maybe she would teach a class."

"Great! She likes to teach."

After dinner all but Barry declined Qwilleran's invitation to have a nightcap at the barn. The innkeeper said he had to pick up his library book and the framed picture of the old hotel. Barry said he had had enough champagne but would like some bottled water. Qwilleran poured Squunk water and introduced him to yet another Moose County specialty.

"What's that on the rug?" the visitor asked.

"A Brazil nut!" Qwilleran exclaimed. "Very odd! The cats are never interested in nuts!"

They sat in the lounge area with their mineral water, and Barry said, "I had a great time tonight! Good food. Great people. Hixie is an interesting woman. How long have you known her?"

"A long time. We met Down Below. I was instrumental in bringing her here; there was a job opening, and she wanted a career change. She has clever ideas and boundless enthusiasm."

"Is she single? Divorced? Any attachments?"

"She was never married, but I don't know about her

present status. She and Dwight have apartments in the same building in Indian Village and frequently attend functions together, but that doesn't mean anything."

"If I invited her to dinner, what would be a good restaurant, other than the Mackintosh Room and the Old Stone Mill?"

"Tipsy's Tavern in Kennebeck," Qwilleran suggested. "It's a roadhouse in a log cabin, established in the 1930s. Good steak and fish."

"Who's Tipsy?"

"That was the name of the original owner's cat, and her portrait, painted in oils, hangs in the main dining room. A few years ago there was fierce controversy about the color of Tipsy's feet. Some said black; some said white . . . That's Moose County for you!"

After the innkeeper had left, Qwilleran scouted the premises for more Brazil nuts and found three—with fang marks. Koko liked oily foods, yet there was no sign of nibbling. . . . Where was that cat? There were sounds of slurping. Koko was on the coffee table, licking snapshots.

"NO!" Qwilleran thundered, and Koko fled the scene of the crime. He had a passion for licking the surface of photographs, and his saliva and rough tongue left ugly splotches. Several prints of the Scottish Gathering were ruined.

It's my fault, Qwilleran thought; I should have put them away. He gave the cats their bedtime snack and escorted them to their quarters on the top balcony. He himself retired to his studio on the first balcony and read from *Domestic Manners of the Americans.* It was good but not good enough to keep him awake, and he was dozing in his chair when the telephone jolted him awake. His watch said almost two o'clock, so it was obviously a wrong number.

He grabbed the handset and snapped a gruff "Yes?"

"Mr. Q, you'll hate me for calling so late." It was Lenny Inchpot, and his voice was heavy with emotion.

Qwilleran felt an uneasiness on his upper lip. "Something wrong?"

"Bad trouble!"

"What happened?"

"I can't tell you on the phone."

"Where are you?"

"At the all-night gas station."

"Come on over. Do you remember how to get here?"

"I remember." Lenny had once delivered a take-out meal from Lois's Luncheonette.

Qwilleran threw the switch that lighted the exterior and went down the ramp to wait. Soon the headlights of a pickup came bobbing through the wooded trail.

He went out to meet it. "Are you okay, Lenny?"

"Shook up, that's all. Oh, God! You won't believe it, Mr. Q!"

"You look pale. Would you like a brandy? Coffee? Food?"

"I don't feel like anything, to tell the truth." In the barn he dropped into a big chair.

"First tell me if Boze reported tonight," Qwilleran said.

Lenny shook his head soberly. "When I finished at midnight, I gave him fifteen minutes and then reported to the manager before heading for home. Employees park in the back lot, which hasn't been paved or lighted yet, so I didn't notice the truck parked next to mine, until a squeaky voice said, 'Hey! Len!' I froze! He called again, and I beamed my flashlight in the cab. It was Boze at the wheel. He told me to get in."

"What was your reaction?"

"Relief! I wasn't angry or anything—just relieved to find him alive. I jumped in beside him, punched his shoulder, and called him a dirty dog. He didn't say anything—just turned on the ignition. Boze never says much. I noticed he was wearing the same T-shirt he wore to toss the caber—and the gold medal around his neck. He looked as if he'd been living in the woods. He's more at home in a cave, you know, than a room with a bed. We were driving toward Chipmunk. There's a bar there that he likes, and I thought we'd talk over a beer, but he turned off on a dirt road, parked under some trees, and turned off the headlights."

"And still he didn't talk?"

"Not a word. It was spooky back there—really dark. Then he turned to me and said, 'Did it get in the paper?' . . . Well, I told him about the splash on the front page, the big headline, the terrific photos! He smiled his dumb smile. I told him we'd been worried when he didn't show up two nights in a row. That's when he said, 'I got another job.' POW! Just like that! It really burned me up, Mr. Q! I'd gone out on a limb to get him into the inn. For Boze to quit without a word was a slap in the face. But I had to be careful. He's touchy. Also big! So I asked him casually what kind of work, and he said he was going to be a bodyguard! Nobody around here ever needed a bodyguard!"

"But stop and think, Lenny. The new gambling casino in Bixby might need a bouncer. The owners might have been at the Highland Games, scouting."

"Yeah . . . well . . . you haven't heard the worst. Before I could think what to say, he blurted out, 'I'm gonna go to Rio. On an airplane. Lotsa fun down there. Easy work. Beaches and carnivals. All that.' Honestly, Mr. Q, I couldn't believe what I was hearing."

Qwilleran stroked his moustache. The possibilities were racing through his mind.

Lenny was saying, "I really thought he was cracking up. So I asked some simple-minded questions, like, when he was flying to Brazil. He said, 'Soon as she sends me the ticket. She's nice. We're gonna have fun. She likes me. I helped her out. Took care of the old guy. Drove her to the airport when I got through work. She told me not to tell anybody. They wouldn't understand.' . . . Oh God! What was he saying? That he killed the jeweler?" Lenny stopped to gulp.

"Take it easy," Qwilleran said. "Did Boze say why she wanted 'the old guy' killed?"

"She said he was sick . . . he was dying . . . he was in pain . . . it would be kind to help him die."

"What did you say, Lenny?"

"What could I say? I felt rotten. Poor Boze! Such an easy make! I just told him I had to go home and get some sleep. I said I have an early class tomorrow. So he drove me back to my truck, and I wished him well in Brazil. I think I told him to send me a postcard. I don't know what I said, Mr. Q. I was really shook up."

"You handled it well under the circumstances," Qwilleran said.

"What do I do now?"

"Tell the story to Allen Barter first thing in the morning. He'll know the proper action to take. It'll be a hard bullet to bite, but you're required to report such information—or be guilty of complicity."

Lenny groaned. "I told you I'm jinxed."

"And I told you not to use that word again! You're like Lois; you always survive setbacks and come out stronger than ever. I'll call Bart at home—early. Meanwhile, you go up to the guestroom on the second balcony and get some sleep. Would you like a warm drink before you turn in? At the risk of sounding like your mother, I recommend cocoa."

eleven

WEDNESDAY, SEPTEMBER 16—*A cat once bitten by a snake will fear even a rope.*

At seven A.M. Qwilleran telephoned G. Allen Barter at home and said in a tone of urgency, "Are you aware that the hero of the Highland Games has been AWOL from his job at the inn? The captain of the desk clerks has a disturbing explanation to relate. It has to do with the Delacamp homicide. You need to hear his tale and take proper action at once."

"I can be in my office by nine o'clock, Qwill."

"Forget the formalities, Bart. Jump into a sweatsuit and drive to my barn. The witness is here, and the murderer is at large in the woods."

Qwilleran knocked on Lenny's door and told him the attorney was on his way. He was not fond of being everybody's uncle, and yet the rising generation seemed to have cast him in that role, unloading their confidential problems and expecting advice. It was partly because of his standing in the community, partly because of his sympathetic mien and willingness to listen. There was also a journalist's need to *hear everything*—and hear it first. He fed the cats and watched them devour their breakfast with all the slurping and gobbling and crunching of ordinary felines. Yet, one of them had licked three snapshots the night before. Koko's raspy tongue had ruined shots of Boze tossing the caber, Boze receiving the gold medal, and Boze riding triumphantly on the shoulders of his teammates. Was it some coincidence? Or was he tuned in to the unknowable? It was not the first time such a mystifying "coincidence" had occurred.

When the attorney arrived, he left him with Lenny and went about his errands. He shopped for Polly's groceries and put the sacks in the trunk of her car in the library parking lot. He killed some time at Eddington's bookstore and found a secondhand book on *How to Trace Your Family Tree*. In mid-morning he dropped in the Dimsdale Diner, where Benny, Doug, Sig, and others in the farming community met to solve the world's problems and drink the world's worst coffee. Disparaging it was an ongoing under-the-table joke. "Brewed from the finest quality of motor sludge" and "Produced and distributed by Pottle's Hog Farm" brought roars of laughter, interrupted only by a bulletin on the radio.

"Police are searching for a local suspect in the Delacamp murder case. No further details have been released at this time."

"Benny did it," said Calvin.

"Spencer did it," said Doug.

Sig suggested it was a police ploy to mislead the real suspect Down Below. "What do you think, Qwill?"

"Time will tell," Qwilleran said.

Next came the weekly luncheon of the Boosters Club in its new venue, the ballroom of the Mackintosh Inn. It was still a soup-and-salad affair served very fast; most members were shopkeepers, managers, and professionals with no time to waste.

Barter was there, and he drew Qwilleran aside to say, "I took the young man to the prosecutor's office to tell his story, and we both decided he should leave town for a few days for his own protection. He can go to his aunt in Duluth."

"How will this be explained to his boss?"

"I had him phone Barry and ask for a week's leave, saying there had been a death in the family and he was needed to help an elderly relative. This whole situation is troubling."

Qwilleran agreed. "The truth, when it comes out, will be painful. They've made Boze such a hero!"

At the tables the conversation was friendly but brief, geared to fit between bites of food before the presiding officer banged the gavel.

Susan Exbridge, the antiques dealer, sat next to Qwilleran and said, "Darling! It's been so long!" Since joining the theatre club she had become dramatic in speech and gesture.

"I've been in Mooseville," he said.

"How's Polly?"

"She's fine. What's new in antiques?"

"I'm liquidating a collection of mechanical banks."

"What are they?"

"Small cast-iron banks for saving coins."

"Expensive?"

"One is valued at fifty thousand."

He took a swallow or two before asking, "What do they look like?"

"Some are cute. Some are ugly. Come and see them at my shop."

BANG! BANG! BANG! The meeting was called to order. The Boosters Club had accepted the responsibility of the Mark Twain Festival, and the various committees were reporting on progress:

About the parade: "The idea is to have characters from Mark Twain stories marching in costume. So far we've signed up Soldier Boy, the horse; Aileen, the dog; Tom Quartz, the cat (to be drawn in a wagon); and more than fifty Tom Sawyers. The question arises: How many clones do we want?"

About the lecture series: "We invited a well-known Mark Twain expert in California, but he's lukewarm. He says he never heard of Pickax and can't find it on the map. Also, his fee is quite high. Question: Should we reconsider? Someone like Jim Qwilleran could probably give the lectures, if he did a little research."

Shouts of "Hear! Hear!"

About the dedication of Mark Twain Boulevard: "We thought to honor the author by naming a historically important, architecturally attractive street after him, but the forty-seven property owners on Pleasant Street are protesting violently to any name change. There was a near-riot at city council meeting last week. We can't name some grubby little backstreet after him, can we? The committee would welcome input."

About the proposed Mark Twain Suite at the Mackintosh Inn: "Well, you all know what happened in the suite a few days ago, virtually under the portrait of the Great Man. The management of the inn deems it inappropriate to draw attention to the presidential suite at this time—probably next year."

About lapel buttons to be sold at the festival: "Unfortunately our fifteen thousand polar bear lapel buttons couldn't be used when the ice festival melted down. We proposed having them reworked with Mark Twain's portrait, but the cost of reworking would be higher than starting from scratch. The committee would welcome ideas for using the polar bear buttons."

A husky man raised a hand and requested the floor.

"The chair recognizes Wetherby Goode."

The WPKX meteorologist said, "As the messenger who brings bad news, I expect to be shot . . . but it's my duty to report that the long-range forecast for October gives thumbs-down to picnics, soccer games, parades, and outdoor festivals. We all remember the freak thaw last February. Everything points to freak weather in October: blizzards, sleet storms, sub-zero temperatures, high winds, and several feet of snow. Need I say more?"

He sat down, amid shouts of "Cancel it! . . . Postpone it! . . . Forget it! . . . Get out the polar bear buttons!"

Then a bell rang, and the sound of scraping chairs and feet running for the exit drowned out the shout of "Meeting adjourned!"

Qwilleran, the only Booster without a demanding schedule, ambled up Main Street to a shop with gold lettering on the window: Exbridge & Cobb, Fine Antiques. The window was always sparkling; the artifacts of brass and mahogany were always polished; and the prices were always high.

"Darling! I didn't expect you so soon!" Susan cried.

"I'll go away."

"No! No! Come into my office and see the collection of banks." She led the way to the rear and unlocked a closet where shelves were lined with nondescript metal objects measuring five or six inches in height and width.

He said, "I want to see the one that's worth fifty thou."

The dealer hesitated. "If you write about these, you can't mention prices or the name of the owner. She's an older woman. The banks were collected by her late husband."

"I didn't say I'd write about them. I just want to see them."

"You're so brutally honest, Qwill."

The bank she showed him was a small iron sculpture of a circus pony and a clown.

"How does it work?" he asked.

"Do you have a penny? Put it in the coin receptacle and turn the crank."

He did as instructed and watched the pony run around a circus ring while the clown deposited the penny in the bank.

Susan explained, "All of these banks have mechanical parts that activate a donkey or elephant or whatever. They became popular in the late nineteenth century when children were taught to save their pennies. This made it fun."

"How many fifty-thousand-dollar banks do you expect to sell in Pickax?"

"None, darling. I'm advertising the rare ones in a national magazine. The others will be sold by telephone auction."

Qwilleran studied the banks in wonderment. There were cats, dogs, monkeys, cows, a whale, and one bust of a Scotsman wearing a Glengarry cap and shoulder tartan. He had a large moustache. He looked amiable.

"He looks just like you, darling. Would you like to buy him?" She placed a coin on the Scot's hand and pressed a lever. He blinked his eyes, raised his arm, and dropped the coin in his pocket.

"What's it worth?"

"Well . . . it's not as old as the others, but it's American and in good condition. The Germans made a bank with a Scotsman who stuck out his tongue and swallowed the coin. Maggie's husband thought it was repulsive."

"Did you say Maggie? Is she selling this collection?"

"I'll phone her and see how much she wants for Kiltie. That's the name of the Scotsman."

Qwilleran fed pennies into the various banks until Susan returned and said, "Maggie said she'll take fifteen hundred for Kiltie. I hope you know that's a steal."

Archly he replied, "I don't want to rob an elderly widow, when she's down to her last diamond-and-pearl choker."

"She likes you! She loves your column!" Susan said. "Also, I told her you're going to help with the telephone auction."

"I don't remember volunteering. However . . . what does it entail?"

"Simply sit at a phone and take bids from collectors all over the United States. With your wonderful voice you can charm the callers into raising their bids. . . . I'll get a box for Kiltie."

· · ·

On the way to the parking lot with the box under his arm, Qwilleran passed the office of Mac-Whannell & Shaw and went in to show them his prize.

"Where'd you get that ugly thing?" Big Mac demanded, then added in a milder tone, "Perhaps I shouldn't say that, because he looks a lot like you."

"Got a dime? I'll show you how it works."

The accountant placed his dime on Kiltie's hand and pressed the lever. The eyes blinked, and the coin disappeared. "Do I get my dime back?"

"Of course not! This is a bank. Are you a bank robber?"

"That's some racket you've got going, Qwill! Let's show it to Gordie." He called his partner on the intercom.

Gordon Shaw was there promptly. "What's going on?"

"Magic!" said Qwilleran.

Another dime disappeared, and the partner hooted with glee. "Go across the street and show it to Scottie!"

The owner of Scottie's Men's Store laughed so hard that his tailor came running from the workroom and happily watched his own dime drop into Kiltie's pocket.

Qwilleran was enjoying it immensely and decided to rook the guys at the newspaper. When he carried the box into the city room the staff was relaxing for a few minutes after putting the Wednesday edition to bed and before starting the Thursday. They gathered around Kiltie and fished for dimes in their change pockets. The managing editor and the women in the feature department joined the fun, and Arch Riker came from his office to investigate the commotion. Kiltie was such a pleasant fellow that no one objected when he pocketed the money, although Riker suggested it would work equally well with pennies.

Junior Goodwinter called it bank robbery Pickax-style. "Instead of robbing the bank, the bank robs you."

Qwilleran was two dollars richer when he left the building, and teasing him about it became a corporate pastime for the rest of the year.

At the barn, where every new acquisition was danger-ous until proved safe, the Siamese sniffed Kiltie's mous-tache, blinking eyelids, and moving hand. Yum Yum soon walked away, but Koko scrutinized the bank in his nearsighted, studious way until suddenly alerted. His neck stretched and ears pricked as he detected activity to the east. Someone was coming up the trail from the di-rection of the art center.

Qwilleran went into the yard to confront the unin-vited visitor when he recognized the ten-year-old boy from the McBee farm.

"Culvert! What a pleasant surprise! I think of you daily when I read my thought-for-the-day."

"Oh," he said.

"What can I do for you?"

"My dad said I could ask you for something."

"And what might that be?"

"Could you get me Boze's autograph? Dad says he works at your hotel."

That posed a problem, and Qwilleran stalled. "It's not my hotel, tell your dad. It belongs to the K Fund. It just happens to be named after my mother."

"Oh," Culvert said dully. Such facts had nothing to do with his urgent mission.

"And it's no longer a hotel; it's an inn, which offers a friendlier kind of hospitality."

"Oh."

"Did you see Boze toss the caber on Saturday?"

He shook his head. "It was in the paper. They talked about it at school."

"Unfortunately Boze isn't working this week, so we'll have to wait and see what happens. How's everything at school?"

"Okay," Culvert said, and ran back down the lane.

After thawing something for his dinner, Qwilleran walked to the Old Stone Church on Park Circle, where the genealogy club met. The Lanspeaks were waiting for him at the side door.

"Everyone's excited about your coming," Carol said.

"Are they expecting me to stand on my head or do impersonations?"

In the fellowship room twenty members were sitting in a circle, and Qwilleran went around shaking hands. He needed no introduction. Everyone glanced at his moustache and said, "I read your column . . . Where do you get your ideas? . . . How are your kitties?" All were his age or older.

After a brief business meeting, a member read a paper on his genealogical research in Ireland, and others spoke about their happy discoveries in family documents, or at the courthouse, or in cemetery records, or in federal military archives.

Finally Larry Lanspeak asked the honored guest if he would say a few words.

You skunk! Qwilleran thought, why didn't you warn me? Nevertheless, he stood up, looked around the circle and blinked his eyes as he considered his chore. (I feel just like Kiltie, he thought.) Then, in his mellifluous lecture-hall voice he began:

"This evening has been an experience that's enlightening, to say the least. I myself am a lost entity wandering in a void—minus relatives, family records, and even an inkling of my father's first name. He died before I was born, and my mother never mentioned his name or those of my grandparents.

"Those of you who have births and deaths inscribed on the flyleaves of family bibles must consider my predicament strange indeed. To me, growing up as the only child of a single parent, there was nothing strange about it at all. It never occurred to me to ask questions, being too busy playing baseball, acting in school plays, doing homework, reading books about dogs and horses, and fighting with my peers.

"My mother died when I was in college, and later all family memorabilia were destroyed in a fire. . . . What can I tell you? We lived in Chicago; my mother's maiden name was Mackintosh; our last name was spelled with a QW. That's all I know. My case rests."

The moment of silence that preceded the burst of applause testified to the deeply touching nature of his confession. One woman sobbed audibly. He acknowledged the response with a sober nod. Actually there had been no fire, but it was not so much a lie as a euphemism for the black period in his life when he lost everything, including his self-esteem.

When the Lanspeaks were driving him home, Carol

said, "Qwill, I didn't know you were such a man of mystery!"

Larry said, "Do you mind if I turn on the eleven o'clock news?"

The lead item was a death notice: "Osmond Hasselrich, eighty-nine, died at Pickax General Hospital tonight after an illness of several weeks. The senior partner of Hasselrich Bennett and Barter had practiced law in Moose County for sixty years. A native of Little Hope, he survived his wife, daughter, and two brothers."

"The end of an era," Larry said. "He was a grand old gentleman! He claimed to be—and I quote—'just a country lawyer but the best goldurned country lawyer you'll ever find!' And he was right!" Then Larry declaimed in his best oratorical style, "Farewell, noble Osmond."

Qwilleran's chief memory of the old man was his custom of serving tea to his clients, pouring it into his grandmother's porcelain cups that rattled in their saucers when he passed them with shaking hands.

When he entered the barn, the Siamese were waiting side by side, solemnly, as if they knew something momentous had happened. Koko ran to the answering machine, where there was a message from the junior partner of HB&B: "Qwill, Osmond has gone! I was with him at the end. There's something he wants you to have. Can you meet me for lunch in the Mackintosh Room tomorrow at twelve? Call my office."

Uncomfortably, Qwilleran thought, He's left me his grandmother's cups and saucers! I made the mistake of admiring them too much.

twelve

THURSDAY, SEPTEMBER 17—*Monkey see, monkey do.*

When Qwilleran came down the ramp in the morning, he saw an unusual spectacle: two cats sitting on their haunches with tails curled and ears at attention, but they were two feet tall, and their ears measured about five inches. Koko and Yum Yum were in the foyer, watching birds through the sidelights, and the morning sun slanted in at a low angle and elongated their shadows on the floor.

Another surprise was in store when he turned on the radio for the hourly newscast:

"A sheriff's deputy was attacked in the woods near the Big B minesite sometime after midnight, while investigating an abandoned pickup registered to John Campbell, a suspect in the local slaying of a Chicago businessman. Deputy Greenleaf was struck on the head by a blunt object. When she regained consciousness, her service revolver was missing. The suspect is now considered armed and dangerous, described as a Caucasian male in his early twenties, six-feet-two, weighing two hundred and fifty pounds. When last seen he was wearing a Moose County Bucks T-shirt."

Qwilleran discussed the item with the Siamese as their heads bent over their breakfast plates: "Boze apparently ran out of gas. Will he use the gun to hijack another vehicle? Do the sport fans know that John Campbell, the alleged attacker, is Boze Campbell, the champion?"

"Yargle" was Koko's comment as he attempted to yowl and swallow at the same time.

At noon Qwilleran met the attorney for lunch at the Mackintosh Room. "Hear the news?" Barter asked. "It puts a new slant on the case. The authorities are smart, though, not to identify the suspect as the caber-tosser. Local sport fans can be fanatical in support of their heroes."

"There'll be a lot of disappointment," Qwilleran added. "My neighbor kid asked me to get Boze's autograph; they'd been talking about him at school."

"Let's hope he's apprehended before he commits any more felonies. Now he's armed."

Qwilleran smoothed his moustache. "Lenny says he's never been out of the county, so I doubt that he'll head for parts unknown to him. He's an experienced backwoodsman, and they're a breed of their own. It's my hunch that he'll hole up in a cave or some kind of impenetrable thicket and use the gun for shooting small game. There's plenty of that around."

"The sheriff's helicopter will be able to spot him," Bart said confidently.

The server brought a glass of red wine and a glass of Squunk water, and the two men toasted the memory of Osmond Hasselrich.

"It was time for him to go," the attorney said. "He was distraught after his daughter's tragic death but kept going for his wife's sake. When she died, though, we knew he wouldn't last long." Barter shook his head. "Osmond had always been my mentor, and in recent years he treated me like a son. I was with him every day at the end. He wanted to discuss his final wishes. Instead of a funeral he wanted a memorial service like Euphonia Gage's, but he wanted it at the Old Stone Church with a solitary bagpiper playing *Loch Lomond* and a few of his favorite hymns. Andrew Brodie was a great friend of his."

"Did Osmond have Scottish blood?"

"He claimed he couldn't find so much as a sheepdog in his ancestry, but he frequently took his wife and daughter to the Highlands and Islands and called himself a closet kiltie."

"What will there be at the memorial service besides music?"

"No eulogies! He said he wanted the reading of 'great words' by 'great voices.' He meant you, Qwill, and Larry and Carol."

"High praise indeed," Qwilleran murmured. "Did he specify the readings?"

"He wanted Carol to read his favorite biblical passage: First Corinthians, chapter thirteen. Larry is to read the words of early statesmen, as in the Declaration of Independence and the Preamble to the Constitution. You are requested to read Robert Burns with a Scottish accent, and also Kipling's poem 'If': 'If you can keep your head when all about you /Are losing theirs.'"

"Any Shakespeare?"

"We discussed it, and the only line he suggested from Shakespeare was: 'The first thing we do, let's kill all the lawyers.' Osmond never lost his wry sense of humor. I think he really had some Scottish blood."

Then lunch was served, and conversation was intermittent. Qwilleran was thinking about the firm of HB&B. Would they drop Osmond's revered name? Would they bring in a new partner? The one in line was a cousin of Wetherby Goode's, Loretta Bunker. The jokesters in Moose County would have a good time with Bennett Barter & Bunker. The prestigious law firm of Goodwinter & Goodwinter had come to an unfortunate end when a third name was proposed.

After lunch Barter retrieved a package he had checked at the front desk. "Osmond thought you should have this," he told Qwilleran.

It was an old-fashioned box-file with metal clasp, leather spine, and boards covered in marbleized paper. The label on the spine read "Klingenschoen Correspondence."

The Thursday paper was due off the presses at two o'clock, and Qwilleran went to the newspaper office to wait for it.

Junior Goodwinter said, "We're running some somber stuff today, but that's the way it works out: the Hasselrich obituary, the assault on the deputy, and the postponement of the Mark Twain Festival. But there's a letter to the editor that will give you a laugh. It's in response to one of your recent columns." He handed over a proof sheet of the letter:

> To the editor: After reading Mr. Q's dissertation on fibs—white, off-white, gray and shades of black, I made a list of twelve little white lies that are in common use:
>
> You look wonderful!
> Don't worry. He doesn't bite.
> A child can assemble it. All that's needed is a screwdriver.
> Guaranteed for life!
> Of course I remember you!
> The chef says the clam chowder is very good today.
> This won't hurt. You'll just feel a little discomfort.
> Drop in any time. You're always welcome.
> The doctor will be with you in just a moment.
> You don't need an umbrella. It's not going to rain.
> This car has been driven only ten thousand miles.
> I love you.
>   —Bob Turmerick

Qwilleran chuckled. "Who is this Turmerick?"

"No one knows him, but the letter came from Sawdust City. I thought you'd enjoy it. . . . Are you covering the play for us tonight?"

Qwilleran went alone to the K Theatre; Polly had another commitment.

The enthusiastic amateurs who auditioned for such

productions were office workers, MCCC students, nurses, commercial fishermen, truck drivers, and waiters who had enjoyed being in school plays and church pageants. As for the audiences, half of them were friends or relatives of the actors; many had never seen players of professional caliber except on TV; many had never seen live theatre.

On the whole, Qwilleran thought, the cast did well. There were no forgotten lines or missed cues. The voice coach had convinced them to project their lines to the show-goers in the back row.

When it was over Qwilleran went home and was writing a review for Friday's deadline when Polly phoned. "How was the play?" she asked.

"Not bad. How was your meeting?"

"The library needs a new furnace. Mr. Hammond came to the meeting himself and convinced the board members that we're only throwing money away on repairs. We're 'spitting into the wind,' he said. The metaphor shocked the ladies into action. They signed a contract without the usual fussing, because of the cold-weather scare."

"Can Hammond have the new equipment installed and operating before the heavy snows and freezing temperature?" Qwilleran asked.

"To tell the truth, Qwill, it's been on order since August. He and I knew it was inevitable, so . . ."

"You practiced a little duplicity."

"Sometimes it's necessary, dear. And I knew the K Fund would help us pay for it. . . . Well, I know you're writing your review, so I won't keep you."

"I'll talk with you tomorrow night after the maiden voyage of the new bookmobile."

"Did you see the list of scheduled stops in today's paper?"

"Yes, and I'll meet it at Ittibittiwassee Estates."

"Good choice. À bientôt."

"À bientôt."

During the phone conversation Koko had been sitting on the box of Klingenschoen correspondence, and now he hunched down on it with his tail elevated like a flag as he went through the motions of digging into the box.

"Okay, we'll have a look," Qwilleran said, "and you can write my review of the play."

He opened it gingerly, as if it might contain the skeleton of a dead mouse, or even a live one. False alarm! The box contained handwritten letters on stationery yellowing with age. The handwriting looked familiar.

"Treat!" he shouted and gave the cats their bedtime snack, then escorted them to the top balcony. When he came down the ramp he was wearing the paisley silk pajamas that Polly had given him for Father's Day, with a mushy card from Koko and Yum Yum. He took time to brew coffee before settling into a lounge chair with the box of old letters.

The handwriting was definitely his mother's. She had been proud of her penmanship: fine pen strokes, slanted, precise, elegant. She had learned it at a private school—somewhere. No one wrote like that these days. Scanning

the sheets he found they had all been written to Aunt
Fanny and dated with the month and day—no year. June
2 was the date on the first one. It was signed "Love from
Annie." His mother's presence haunted the page as he
began to read, and shivers traveled up and down his
spine.

Dear Fanny—

How's everything? Are you having fun? Do you
like Atlantic City as much as you thought you
would? I know you don't have time to write letters,
so don't bother to answer this, but . . . I have
NEWS! I told you my parents wanted me to go back
to Des Moines and work in Dad's office, but I adore
Chicago TOTALLY, and after slaving for four years
as an English major, I'd jump off a bridge before I'd
work in an insurance office, and I told them so. It
didn't go over big! Dad is hopping mad about my
moving to Chicago, and Mother goes along to keep
the peace. She's afraid to cross him. She says she
loves him. I guess I don't understand LOVE. And
she doesn't understand why I don't want to marry
her best friend's son. Dad would take him into the
business and we'd all live happily ever after. But I
can't STAND the guy! He's so DULL, and his eyes
are too close together. (You know what you and I
used to say about THAT!)

So here I am, and my wildest dream has come
true—a job in the PUBLIC LIBRARY! I get a
clerk's salary because I don't have a degree in library
science, but—just between you and me—I do everything the librarians do. But that's okay. I love the

work TOTALLY. With my first paycheck I made a down payment on a secondhand upright. You never heard me play the piano, but I think I'm really pretty good. Just for fun—to make Dad hit the ceiling—I asked him to ship my baby grand. Fat chance! . . . I have a small apartment, and the girl across the hall is nice—Sue Ellen, from Tennessee, pronounced Tinnissee. We go to plays and concerts together—just a couple of country girls whooping it up in the big city.

Love from Annie

Qwilleran huffed into his moustache. So his grandfather was in insurance! In Des Moines! That might be the place to start checking county records. Even if it proved a dead end it might be worth the trip . . . But what about this twenty-two-year-old who turned out to be his MOTHER? (Her letter had him thinking in capital letters.) Lady Anne was so CALM and SENSIBLE! He read the next letter, dated June 10:

Dear Fanny—

Want to hear some FABULOUS news? Sue Ellen and I went to see a Russian play—strictly for our education. It was GRIM! But the actor who played the male lead was enthralling—TOTALLY! Glorious voice—expressive hands—and good-looking, even with a Russian beard. After the final curtain we wondered if we dared to go backstage and compliment him. We giggled about it and then said, "Oh, let's!"

Well! He was totally CHARMING and even in-

vited us to have a drink! We went with him to a little bistro, and I don't mind telling you, we were
both weak in the knees! I didn't sleep a wink that
night, I was so overwhelmed! And that was only
the beginning! The next day he phoned me at the
library! And I met him for drinks after the play—
every night for the rest of the run. It's a road company, and they had to move on. We had a LOVELY
farewell date, and he promised to write, but I'm
afraid to hope. Keep your fingers crossed for me,
Fanny.

Love from Annie

Qwilleran returned the letters to the box, all the while
marveling that this giddy young female could metamor-
phose into a suave, sophisticated parent who never said
"totally."

thirteen

FRIDAY, SEPTEMBER 18—*To live a long life, eat like a cat and drink like a dog.*

It was a beautiful day for the ride to Ittibittiwassee Estates. The bookmobile was due to arrive at eleven-thirty, and Qwilleran went a little early. Already residents were gathering on the lawn in front of the building, and there was an air of excitement. Some sat on the park benches that lined the circular driveway. One group sat in a circle of lawn chairs, and bursts of laughter came from the five women and three men. Among them were Homer and Rhoda Tibbitt, the Cavendish sisters, and Gil MacMurchie.

"This sounds like a lively bunch," he said as he approached the circle. "What kind of jokes are you telling?"

Jenny and Ruth Cavendish had been his neighbors in Indian Village, and he had made himself a hero by saving one of their cats from strangulation behind the washing machine. They were retired academics who had enjoyed illustrious careers Down Below and had returned to their native county. Ruth, the tall one, was a born leader.

"Gil, bring another chair! Qwill, sit down. You have stumbled into a board meeting of a new publishing house, The Absolutely Absurd Press, Inc. We publish only absolutely absurd titles."

He sat down. "Could you give me an example?"

"Our first will be *The Complete Works of Shakespeare in One Volume, Large Print Edition.*" She paused for his amused reaction. "The next will be *The Collected Love Poems of Ebenezer Scrooge.* Several other titles are—"

She was interrupted by a general shout. "Here comes the bus!"

"Rhoda," she said, "make a list of titles for Qwill. He might use them in his column."

The board members and other waiting book-lovers swarmed toward the driveway. The white bookmobile that had looked like a laundry truck was now a mobile mural of the county. On the boarding side a billboard-size painting was a panorama of woods with a startled deer, rocky pastures dotted with sheep, and a shafthouse towering above an abandoned minesite. On the driver's side, surf pounded on a sandy shore; seagulls soared above a beached boat and drying fishnets; a lighthouse stood on a distant promontory.

The vehicle was staffed by two energetic young women from the library, who handed out shopping bags full of books to be carried into the building. Then browsers went aboard, including Qwilleran.

The two staffers sat with backs to the windshield, ready to check out individual choices.

He asked, "Which one of you drives this thing?"

"I do," said one.

"Is it tricky?"

"Only going around corners." The women looked at each other and laughed.

"What places do you visit, besides the Estates?"

"Schools, churches, nursing homes, day-care centers, hospitals. We even stop at the grocery store at Squunk Corners."

"What kinds of books do you bring in those tote bags?"

"It depends. Here they like biography, history, humor, inspiration, nature, large print, mysteries. Other places like cookbooks, juveniles, romance, westerns, Nancy Drew . . ."

Rhoda Tibbitt picked up a book her husband had special-ordered: a new biography of Thomas Jefferson. Then the half hour was up; the transactions were completed; and the management of the residence invited Qwilleran and the two staffers to come indoors for a little lunch. First the driver took the large vehicle away from the front door of the building—the "ambulance entrance," as the residents called it. She drove it down the hill to the foot of the circular driveway and then ran back up the hill.

"We have five more stops to make this afternoon," she explained.

"Oh, to be able to run up a hill!" one of the watchers exclaimed.

"Oh, to be able to run *anywhere!*" said another.

In the dining room they were served quickly—a sandwich and a cup of soup—while the resident librarian told them about in-house activities. There was a workshop for training tutors to teach adults to read. She said, "Avid readers take great pleasure in teaching others to read. It's an adventure for both teacher and student."

When it was time to leave, Qwilleran carried out the bags of books being returned, and the driver ran down the hill to bring the vehicle to the door. The Cavendish sisters sent their love to Polly and asked about the health of Brutus and Catta. Rhoda gave Qwilleran a list of absurd titles and urged him to add a few of his own.

Before he could scan the list, a scream came from the foot of the hill, and the driver came running and waving her arms. All heads turned in her direction. The book-mobile was nowhere in sight.

"A big man came out of the woods!" she gasped. "He had a gun! He made me give him the keys!"

Qwilleran shouted, "Somebody call the sheriff—quick! And somebody call the library!" He himself hurried to his van and called the newspaper. Patrons of the bookmobile stood about in a daze; others swarmed out of the building. They were saying:

"Must be the fella that stole the deputy's gun!"

"He's wanted for murder!"

"He won't get far with that conspicuous jalopy!"

"He's desperate! He'll ditch it and steal something else."

And Homer Tibbitt said, "Maybe he just likes to read."

Distant sirens came closer.

Qwilleran drove the library staffers back downtown, along with the bags of books that were being returned. He said nothing, but he was peeved. He had intended to write a thousand words on bookmobiling for his Tuesday column, but the hijacking had killed the idea. It would appear as crime news in Monday's edition.

It was a bizarre story that would appeal to the media Down Below. Locals would be fearful; the man was armed and must be a maniac even to conceive of such a caper. And the concept of a felon riding around with several hundred books would tickle the jokers in the coffee shops. "Only in Moose County!" they would say, slapping their thighs.

By the time Qwilleran reached the barnyard, a WPKX news bulletin announced: "A suspect wanted for murder has highjacked the Pickax library's bookmobile at gunpoint this afternoon while it was making a scheduled stop at Ittibittiwassee Estates. Roadblocks have been set up in three counties. The stolen vehicle is easy to identify, being thirty feet long and painted with murals of Moose County landscape. Anyone seeing it should call the sheriff's department and avoid approaching the hijacker."

The Siamese were having their afternoon nap on the bar stools when Qwilleran arrived, and they slept through his conversation with the director of the library:

"Polly! Just phoning to see if you had a heart attack."

"Qwill! Could you ever, in your wildest dreams, imagine such a ludicrous situation?"

"He can't get far. The sheriff's helicopter will be scanning the highways and back roads."

"Too bad we didn't have BOOKMOBILE painted on the roof in large letters," she said with a touch of whimsy.

"The back roads have overhanging trees. It wouldn't help."

"Thanks for driving the girls back downtown, Qwill."

"Keep your radio turned on."

Qwilleran prepared coffee, changed into a jumpsuit, and stayed close to the radio. Within an hour there was another bulletin:

"The sheriff's ground patrol, directed by the helicopter surveillance detail, has located the hijacked bookmobile, earlier reported stolen. It was found wrecked on an unimproved road in Chipmunk Township. The hijacker is at large, and motorists are warned to keep car doors locked and to avoid picking up hitchhikers. The suspect, wanted for murder, is described as two hundred and fifty pounds, armed and dangerous. The wrecked vehicle, carrying hundreds of books belonging to the Pickax public library, is on its side in a ditch."

Qwilleran's phone rang immediately.

"Qwill! Did you hear?"

"I heard!"

"What an incredible mess! Can you imagine the condition of the books?"

"Is there anything I can do?"

There was no answer.

"Polly! Is there anything I can do?"

"I'm thinking . . . Gippel's Garage can rescue the bus. But we should salvage the books first."

"What can I do?"

"Ernie Kemple will line up his Handy Helpers. Those kids love an emergency like this. But we'll need lots of book crates in a hurry. Liquor cartons are good . . ."

"How many do you need?"

In the next few hours Qwilleran canvassed drug stores, bars, and food markets and delivered a small mountain of

cartons to the back door of the library. When he returned
to the barn in time to clean up for Susan's auction, the
Siamese were furious. The inside of the barn looked like
the inside of the ditched bookmobile. They had not been
fed!

For that matter, neither had Qwilleran, and he had
only half an hour to report to the antique shop. His pri-
orities were clear. He fed the cats.

At ten-thirty P.M. the interior of Exbridge &
Cobb was brightly lighted, although the sign on
the door said CLOSED. A few curious passersby stood on
the sidewalk, gawking. In the main shop they could see
two women sitting at telephones and a man standing at a
chalkboard; in the annex others were eating and drinking and having a good time. "That's Mr. Q," the gawkers
said to each other as he rapped on the front door.

Susan Exbridge admitted him. "Darling! You're always
so punctual!"

"I'm also hungry. I didn't have time for dinner."

"Go into the annex. Maggie has prepared a feast."

The hostess was wearing her usual black, flecked with
cat hair. Her arms were loaded with gold bangles, and her
chest was loaded with pearls. "Here he is!" she cried. "Let
me give him a hug! . . . Would you like wine or coffee,
Qwill?"

"Food!"

Besides the silver coffee service and the cut glass de-
canters there were platters of cheeses and cold cuts.
Susan briefed him while he satisfied his hunger.

"The phones have been open since nine; midnight is

the cut-off. You'll be taking calls during the last hour. Dr. Diane will be at the table with you; Dwight Somers will be at the chalkboard."

"Back up!" he said. "I don't know the basics. How does this thing work?"

She explained. "When a call comes through—from Maine or New Orleans or Los Angeles—you get the caller's name and phone number and the catalogue number of the bank he's interested in. Then you consult the chalkboard and give the amount of the latest bid. The caller may raise it or hang up. If the bid is raised, you call it out to Dwight, and he updates the board."

Dr. Diane said, "I've done this before and found that some calls come from practical jokers or cranks or lonely folks who just want to talk. Tell them three calls are waiting, ask to be excused, and hang up."

"Legitimate bidders," said Susan, "may want additional information, such as dimensions, condition, date, name of maker, or description of bank. Consult your printout and answer their questions."

Qwilleran said, "I can't believe the eyes and ears of the nation are focused on Pickax, 400 miles north of everywhere!"

"You wait and see," said Maggie. "Mr. Sprenkle belonged to an international bank club."

At eleven o'clock Qwilleran and the doctor went to the phone table, and Dwight went to the chalkboard.

The lines had been comfortably busy for the first two hours, Susan said, but the action would build up as the deadline approached. A speaker phone had been set up, and just before midnight she would call a 900 number, and Washington Naval Observatory Time would be announced every five seconds. "That way there'll be no arguments when we cut off the bidding."

Qwilleran's phone rang, and his first call came from Austin, Texas, inquiring about the Butting Ram bank. Qwilleran described the movement for him: "Put coin on limb of tree and press lever . . . ram butts coin into bank . . . a small boy thumbs his nose."

It was in good condition, valued at six thousand; the highest bid was five. The caller raised it five hundred.

A collector in Buckhead, Georgia, called back several times and raised his bid on the Circus Pony bank whenever someone had topped him.

Although most of the callers were men, the wife of a banker in Reno, Nevada, wanted to buy her husband a birthday gift. "Do you think he would like a mechanical bank?"

"I'm sure he would. There's one called the Magic Bank. The cashier takes the coin and disappears with it into a bank vault."

"How charming!" she said. "How old is it? He's not too fond of old things."

"It's dated 1873. Would you like to make a bid? The highest we have is four thousand, although it's valued at sixty-five hundred."

"How big is it?"

"Six inches high. That's approximately the usual size."

"I see . . . Are you an antiques dealer? I love talking to you. You have such a delicious voice."

Crisply Qwilleran said, "A bid for forty-five hundred has just come in on the other line. Better make up your mind."

She offered forty-seven-fifty, and Dwight said, "Qwill, you're a rascal."

"She was holding up the line!"

The phones rang incessantly as the deadline approached, and Dwight was busy with the chalk and eraser. With only five minutes to go, Buckhead made another bid on the Circus Pony. He also inquired about less valuable banks, bidding a hundred dollars here and a hundred dollars there. He was stalling. Qwilleran looked at Dwight and shrugged. The speaker phone was beeping away the seconds. At the stroke of midnight all bids were cut off. Buckhead had his Circus Pony for forty-five thousand. Everyone in the shop applauded.

The Siamese, without help from the Washington Naval Observatory, knew that their bedtime snack was seventy-four minutes past due, and they met Qwilleran at the kitchen door, scolding and lashing their tails.

"All right! All right!" he said. "I was helping an elderly widow who loves cats! Try to be a little understanding, a little more flexible."

As he watched them devour their Kabibbles, he reflected that it had been an eventful day in every way: the hijacking of the bookmobile, the coast-to-coast telephone auction, and even the mad scramble for cardboard cartons for the library—not to mention the debut of the Absolutely Absurd Press, Inc. He had not yet read the list of proposed titles.

He found it in one of his pockets:

Everything You Wanted to Know About Ravens, by
   Edgar Allan Poe.

A *Revised History of the World,* by Lewis Carroll.
Painting by Numbers, with foreword by Leonardo.
How to Make Lasting Friendships, by Richard III.
Bedtime Stories for Tiny Tots, illustrated by Hierony-
    mus Bosch.

The last one was undoubtedly Homer Tibbitt's contribution: *How to Get Away with Anything,* by Mayor Gregory Blythe.

After a few chuckles Qwilleran was feeling relaxed
enough to retire, but first he would read a couple of in-
stallments of the Annie-Fanny correspondence. Next
was the letter dated June 24:

Dear Fanny—

Miracle of miracles! My actor didn't write to me,
but he phoned every week from a different city!
The tour ended in Denver, and he called to say he
was coming back to Chicago. He said life had been
barren without me!

So now he's here and hoping for work, but there's
not much opportunity in his field. He says he's willing to sell neckties at Marshall Field until something turns up. Fanny, you can't believe how
HAPPY I am! I'll send you a snapshot of him when
I finish the roll on my camera. Without the Russian
beard he's really handsome. In my weekly letter to
Mother I broke the good news, and her reply was,
"Dad warns you not to get serious about an actor."
Wouldn't you know? What does he understand
about LOVE?

I'll send you a snapshot of Dana as soon as I finish

the roll in my camera. His last name is Qwilleran, spelled with a QW. He says it's Danish. Be happy for me, dear Fanny. I'm ECSTATIC!

Love from Annie

Qwilleran huffed into his moustache. His male parent should have had sense enough to stay in New York. With his handsome looks, charming personality, and glorious voice he could have been the John Barrymore of his generation. The next letter, dated August 22, was a short one. He read it.

Dear Fanny,

We've decided to get married! Isn't that exciting? I phoned Mother to share the good news, and what an explosion! Totally! Dad got on the line and said he didn't want his daughter marrying an unemployed actor. I told him I had to live my own life. He said, "Then live it your way, but don't come crying to me for help when he can't support you!" I said, "If necessary I can support both of us" and hung up. I knew that would be his reaction, but I don't care. I won't let it put a wet blanket on a joyous occasion. Think good thoughts, Fanny. I know you're on my side.

Love from Annie

"The plot thickens!" Qwilleran said as he replaced the letters in the file.

fourteen

SATURDAY, SEPTEMBER 19—*The fish dies because he opens his mouth too much.*

With his first cup of coffee Qwilleran felt the urge to read another Annie-Fanny letter. He would read only one, he promised himself. It was dated September 30.

Dear Fanny—

We did it! We're married! Dana is impulsive, and I like to make quick decisions, so we simply went across the state line to a place where a couple can get the knot tied without red tape. (Knot! Tape! Ha ha! Don't mind me. I'm tipsy with bliss!) I never wanted a big wedding, although Mother had dreams of seeing me in Grandmother's wedding dress with a ten-foot train and eight bridesmaids in floppy hats. And, of course, a reception for two hundred guests! I knew, and she knew, that Dad would never foot the bill for such an extravaganza.

So here we are, married and TOTALLY happy! My apartment is rather snug for two—unless they're madly in love. Someday we'll have a lovely house in the suburbs, and a garden, and a car, and an attached garage. Dana is working part-time at Marshall Field, and the library gave me a token raise, and we're saving our pennies.

Want to hear something I did that was naughty? I sent my parents a note (signed Annie Qwilleran) telling them that they now had a son-in-law. I couldn't resist telling them he's a tie salesman. I knew Dad would burst a blood vessel. Of course, he wouldn't let Mother acknowledge my note. I don't care. If they don't need a daughter, I don't need parents.

Love from Annie

When Qwilleran returned the letter to the file, Koko was sitting on the library table, paying no attention to the mechanical bank, which was supposed to be his toy. As usual, he showed more interest in the spalted maple box, sniffing the little knob on the lid and pawing the decorative motifs created by flaws in the wood. One was like the outline of a mouse trapped beneath the waxy surface of the box; another looked somewhat like a bee.

"Cats! Unpredictable!" Qwilleran muttered as he thawed a roll for his breakfast. A phone call from Celia Robinson interrupted.

"Chief, sorry to bother you," she said, "but I need to discuss something."

"Shoot!"

"It's about Nora, my helper. I was telling her about

Short & Tall Tales and how you're collecting stories about Moose County—some true, some legends. She said she has a story to tell that actually happened."

"How long ago? Do you know the nature of it?"

"She wouldn't tell me, but she'd like you to hear it. She'd love to see it in your book. She was thrilled, you know, when the paper used her letter."

"It's a heady feeling to see your words in print for the first time. I'll listen to her tale." He never said no to a story; it might be a gem.

"I don't want her to waste your time. It may not be worth anything. She's just a simple country woman, you know." Then she added with a laugh, "Like me."

"You're worth three city women, Celia. Tell you what! Some day when Nora's making a delivery for you, I'll see what's on her mind."

"Wonderful! I'm making beef pot pies today. Shall I make an extra one for you? Also mincemeat tarts?"

"Keep talking."

Celia laughed merrily. "Nora could deliver them this afternoon."

"I'll be gone all day. How about tomorrow morning?"

"She goes to church."

An appointment was made for Sunday afternoon, and Qwilleran went up the ramp to dress, feeling he had made a good deal.

The autumn color in Moose County was at its peak. Gold, red, bronze, coral, maroon—all accenting the groves of dark, dense evergreens. This was the weekend when everyone took to the highways with cameras. Qwilleran, Polly, and the Rikers planned to do the tour and stop for lunch at Boulder House Inn on the north shore. They assembled in Indian Village and rode in Qwilleran's van, which offered a wider view than Arch's four-door.

Polly was looking unusually jaunty in a beige corduroy suit, black beret, and beige-and-black scarf featuring Chinese calligraphy.

Mildred said, "I love your scarf, Polly! You didn't get that around here."

"Thank you. It's from the Boston Museum of Art."

"I hope you know what it says," Arch warned.

"Happiness, harmony, and health—or something like that. All good things, I assure you."

They proceeded to crisscross the county on country roads, driving slowly, gasping at spectacular autumn views, taking snapshots of the most brilliant color. Conversation was limited. "Oh, look at that! . . . Did you ever see anything so beautiful? . . . Breathtaking! . . . Better than ever this year!"

"Why is traffic so light?" Polly wondered. "Usually the roads are crowded on the big weekend."

"Everyone's at home watching the ball game on TV," Arch suggested with his usual cynicism.

The weathered gray shafthouses stood like lonely sentinels in the lush landscape. Each had its history: a cave-in, a mine explosion, a murder. Polly said, "Maggie insists there's a subterranean lake under the Big B."

At the Boulder House Inn their reservation was for one-thirty, giving them time for a walk on the beach. In a few weeks the sand would be buried under three feet of snow. Indoors, to their surprise, the dining room was half empty.

"We've had several cancellations," the innkeeper said. "Just spread a rumor about a killer on the loose, and folks lock themselves in the bathroom."

At a table in the window overlooking the lake Mildred said, "Let's not ruin our lunch by talking about the terrorist in our midst."

"I have good news," said Polly. "After the Cavendish sisters moved out, I worried about getting a noisy neighbor. The walls are deplorably thin! Well, yesterday the new owner came into the library and introduced himself. He's a rare book dealer from Boston!"

"You can't get anyone quieter!" Arch said cheerfully.

"He does mail-order business from his home and is having shelves installed on all the walls. Until his furniture and books arrive he's staying at the Mackintosh Inn."

"What's he like?" Mildred asked eagerly. She was always looking for interesting guests to invite to dinner.

Polly said he was middle-aged, nice-looking, soft-spoken, and quite charming. "Of course, he's tremendously knowledgeable. I expect to learn a lot from him. He specializes in incunabula."

Qwilleran huffed into his moustache and decided, then and there, to close the barn for the winter and move back into his condo, but he said to the group, "I have some news for you, too. The Cavendish sisters, the Tibbitts, and a few others at Ittibittiwassee Estates have organized what they call The Absolutely Absurd Press, Inc., and I have a list of the absurd titles they propose to publish." He read the list, pausing after each title for the amused response—sometimes a giggle, sometimes a guffaw. "I'd also like to add one of my own: *Five Easy Piano Pieces for the Index Finger.*"

The laughter was spontaneous, followed by thoughtful silence as three minds went into gear.

"No hurry," Qwilleran told them. "You have until four o'clock."

By the time coffee and dessert were served, Polly had proposed *Recipes for Entertaining* by Lucrezia Borgia.

Arch's contribution was *My Secret Life as a Pussycat* by King Kong.

Mildred said that books on food were always popular and suggested *Ichabod Crane's Low-Fat Cookbook*.

The two men looked at each other mischievously. "Remember Ichabod?" they said in unison.

Mildred clapped her hands. "Is this another story about your misspent youth?" Whenever the foursome met, Qwilleran and Arch reminisced about growing up in Chicago.

"We were reading Washington Irving that year, and we called our English teacher Ichabod because he was tall and skinny," said Qwilleran. "He was a joker and played tricks on his students when giving tests. We had a great desire to get back at him. . . . Remember that school, Arch?"

"It was an old one and about ready to be torn down. They don't build them like that any more, with the first floor way off the ground."

"The way it happened," Qwilleran went on, "we had to report to room 109 for an English test after lunch, and we got there early. Somehow we got the idea of going in, throwing the bolt on the door, and locking everybody out. Then we went out the window and dropped down on the ground, about six feet. By the time we brushed ourselves off and came in the front door, the whole class was standing in the hall, and the teacher was running around trying to get a janitor with a ladder. The window was wide open, of course."

"Were you ever found out?" Mildred asked.

"Oh, he knew we did it. We were the only kids in the class smart enough to think of it. But he had a sense of humor."

Mildred said, "I wish I'd known you then!"

"I'm glad I didn't!" Polly said.

Qwilleran returned his passengers to Indian Village, dropping the Rikers at The Birches and driving Polly to The Willows.

"Will you come in to say something friendly to Brutus and Catta?" she asked.

"Just for a while. Does your new neighbor have cats?"

"No, but he offered to take care of mine whenever I need to be out of town. He's a very thoughtful person. He brought me this scarf, which I thought was an unusually lovely gesture."

"What's his name?"

"Kirt Nightingale."

"What's his real name?"

"Oh, Qwill! You're always so suspicious!"

"Does he know about our ten-foot snowdrifts and wall-to-wall ice?"

"Oh, yes! He grew up here. His relatives have moved

away, but he has fond memories of winters in Moose
County."

"Perhaps he'd like to join the curling club."

As soon as Qwilleran arrived home he telephoned Pat O'Dell, Celia Robinson's husband,
who ran a janitorial service. He asked to have Unit Four
at The Willows cleaned for immediate occupancy.

"Is it cold feet you're gettin' now?" Pat asked in his lilt-
ing Irish brogue.

"You might say that, Pat. Wetherby Goode predicts
November weather for October."

"Sure, a' it's only one man's opinion, I'm thinkin'. But
a pleasure it'll be to do whatever you want."

While hanging up the receiver Qwilleran noticed that
the lid was off the turned maple box and the pennies
were gone. A quick glance revealed the two culprits on
the fireplace cube, looking down on the scene of the
crime. Koko looked proud of himself; Yum Yum looked
guilty.

"You scalawags!" Qwilleran scolded fondly. "One of
you is a bank robber, and the other is a petty thief."

She had not gone far with her loot; the pennies were
not shiny enough to appeal to her exquisite taste. They
were on the rug nearby. What interested Qwilleran was
Koko's motive: curiosity about its contents? His catly response to a challenge? He had found out how to clamp
his jaws around the knob and lift the well-fitting lid with
a vertical jerk of the head. Smart cat! He had been obsessed with the problem, and now that it was solved, he
would walk away and forget it with his tail held high.

Qwilleran himself was becoming obsessed with the Klingenschoen file. Now he understood why he had never received birthday presents from grandparents, while his friend Archie boasted about getting a cowboy suit and even a two-wheel bike!

The next letter was dated October 10:

Dear Fanny—

Thank you for the gorgeous wedding gift! We're putting it away until we have our house in the suburbs. I can picture it on a console table in the foyer or on the fireplace mantel. All that is in the future—not too distant, I hope. Right now we have to think about Dana's career. Shall we give up our jobs and move to New York where there are plenty of auditions? Or stay here where I have steady income and a promise of promotion? Although Dana is doing well at the store, his heart isn't in retailing. He could make better money as a manufacturer's rep, but I'd hate to have him on the road all the time. What kind of life is that for two people so much in love? We read the want ads every day and hope—and hope—and hope. Dana isn't quite as optimistic as I am, but I know something wonderful is just around the corner.

Love from Annie

A question arose in Qwilleran's mind. What was the gorgeous wedding gift? All the time he was growing up in a respectable townhouse apartment with a foyer and a fireplace, he had never seen such an impressive object, or had paid no juvenile attention. Annie might describe it in a later letter: a crystal vase, a silver bowl, a porcelain figurine . . . He went on to October 22:

Dear Fanny—

Can you stand some terrifically good news? If I sound incoherent it's because I'm tipsy with delight! I've just found out I'm PREGNANT! Dana is sort of stunned. They laughed at me at the library because I immediately checked out an armful of books on parenting. Speaking of parents, I dashed off a note to Mother, but it was returned unopened. Too bad. Some mother/daughter talk would be comforting right now. You are my dearest friend, Fanny. If the baby is a girl, I'll name her after you. If it's a boy, Dana can name him. Frankly, he would be more enthusiastic if he had a decent job, preferably with a repertory acting company. I wish you could see him on the stage, Fanny. He's so talented! It breaks my heart to see him so frustrated. I try to make him feel that he's loved, no matter what. We have each other, and that's what matters, and soon we'll be THREE! Can you believe it?

Love from Annie

After reading the letter he rejoiced that he was not named Francesca Qwilleran, or even Fanny Qwilleran. The next letter was short, but he was limiting himself to two at a sitting. "Goodnight, Annie," he said as he closed the clasp on the box-file.

fifteen

SUNDAY, SEPTEMBER 20—*Contented cows give the best milk.*

Qwilleran was accustomed to spending Saturday and Sunday with Polly, but this weekend she needed a day to do things around the house, to catch up with correspondence, to organize her winter wardrobe. Qwilleran said he understood—and called a friend to have Sunday brunch at Tipsy's Tavern in Kennebeck.

It was a no-frills, limited-menu roadhouse in a sprawling log cabin, serving the best steak and the best fish. A recent innovation was a Sunday brunch offering the best ham and eggs and country fries and the best flapjacks with homemade sausage patties.

Wetherby Goode, the WPKX meteorologist, met him at Tipsy's. He said, "Lots of vacant tables, considering the usual popularity of this brunch."

"The fugitive scare," Qwilleran surmised. "Yesterday we took the color tour, and there was hardly anyone on the road. But the autumn color was magnificent—best ever!"

"Moose County has always had better color than Lockmaster." Wetherby was a native of Horseradish, a town in the adjoining county.

"We have more trees," Qwilleran explained. "After the lumbering companies had cleared the forests a century ago, the Klingenschoen family bought up huge tracts of worthless land and left it to reforest itself. Now the K Fund has it in conservancy, safe from developers who would use it for resort hotels, golf courses, race tracks, mobile home parks, and—God forbid!—asphalt plants. The streams are full of fish, and the woods are full of wildlife."

"The Klingenschoens weren't in lumbering or mining or quarrying. Where did they get their money?"

"Don't ask."

The ham was succulent; the eggs were fried without crusty edges or puddles of grease; the country fries had skins-on flavor and were toasty brown.

Wetherby asked, "When are you closing the barn? You'd better move to The Willows before the first blizzard." He occupied Unit Three.

"We have a new neighbor in Unit Two," Qwilleran said. "Have you met him?"

"No, but I've seen his car. Massachusetts tags."

"He's a rare book dealer from Boston. His name is Kirt Nightingale."

"'Hail to thee, blithe spirit! Bird thou never wert.'" The weatherman always enlivened his predictions with snatches of poetry or songs.

"Wrong bird," said Qwilleran. "It was written to a sky-lark."

"Whatever. It was Keats at his best."

"Sorry, friend. Wrong poet. Shelley wrote it. But speaking of blithe spirits, do you think Amanda will be able to unseat the mayor?"

"Absolutely! She's tough! She's honest! She's a Good-winter! And some of us have talked her into adopting a cat from the animal shelter—to improve her image."

Nora was expected to arrive at the barn with the beef pot pie at three o'clock. While waiting, Qwilleran read another Annie-Fanny letter, dated November 1:

Dear Fanny—

Just a brief note to thank you for your enthusiasm about our baby and also for the darling booties. They're the first item in our layette. It's a long wait, but I'm making plans. I sold my piano to make room for a crib, but that's all right. I'll have a baby grand someday. Meanwhile, I'm reading classic literature for half an hour every evening, hoping to give my baby a love of good writing. I love the story of King Arthur and his court, and if my baby is a boy, I'm going to call him Merlin. Don't you think that's a beautiful name. His middle name will be James, which I think is very noble. Then my pet name for him will be Jamie. Forgive me for rambling on, but I know you're interested.

Love from Annie

Qwilleran groaned as he recalled his youthful embarrassment over those names. "Merlin" was the name on his report card (that was bad enough) but it was his friend Archie who spread the vile lie that he was called "Jamesy" at home. There had been many a fistfight and many a trip to the principal's office.

At three o'clock Celia phoned to say that Nora was on her way with the beef pot pie and some other goodies. "And I just wanted to tell you, Chief, that she has a terrible case of stage fright. You're so famous, and the barn is so big, and your moustache is so—"

"Threatening," he said. "Thanks for tipping me off. I'll try not to growl at her."

He planned an informal chat at the snack bar, with a glass of apple cider. He would introduce the Siamese and let her stroke Yum Yum. He would show her the mechanical bank and give her a coin to deposit; it always amused visitors.

When the red car pulled into the barnyard he went out to meet it and carry the cartons into the kitchen. "Make yourself at home," he said casually. She stood rooted to one spot and gazed around the immense interior in awe and a little fear.

"Do you like apple cider?" he asked.

"Yes, sir," she said.

"Sit down at the snack bar, and we'll have a glass of cider and talk."

"Excuse me, sir, what is that thing?" She pointed to Kiltie, and he explained the bank and gave her a penny to deposit.

"Yow!" came a loud comment from the top of the refrigerator.

"Excuse me, sir, is that a cat?"

"Yes, he's a male Siamese—very smart. He wants you
to start telling your tale. . . . Where did it take place?"

"Do you know Ugley Gardens, sir?"

"I've seen it on the county map. It's spelled U-g-l-e-y."

"Yes, sir. That was a man's name, Oliver Ugley. He had
acres and acres of land, and he rented it to poor farmers.
Farm families came from the Old Country to have a good
life, but the soil was no good, and it was swampy. All
they could raise was turnips. They lived in huts and
didn't have anything to do with. They worked very
hard."

Qwilleran nodded. He had heard about Ugley Gardens. It had been called "the last pocket of deprivation in
Moose County" until the K Fund acquired it and turned
it around. The land was tiled for drainage, and goat-
farming was introduced; the huts were replaced by pre-
fabricated housing; and the families became citizens of a
community.

He asked, "Did your story take place before the goats
came?"

"Yes, sir."

"How did you know about it?"

"I lived there and met a girl at prayer meeting. Her
name was . . . Betsy."

"Was there a church at Ugley Gardens?"

"No, sir. Families just got together and sang hymns."

"Was there something special about Betsy?"

"Yes, sir. She was oldest of six kids and had to stay
home and help her mother. She never went to school."

Qwilleran thought, This doesn't sound real in today's world; it's a fantasy—a fiction. He said, "Don't wait for me to ask questions. Just go on with your story."

"Yes, sir. When Betsy was thirteen she heard about a hotel that hired farm girls to cook and clean because they were hard workers, so she ran away from home. It was a nice job, cleaning rooms and making beds. She slept in the basement and got all her meals. One day the housekeeper told her to take some more towels to a man in one of the rooms. He was a nice man. He said, 'You're a pretty girl. Sit down and talk to me.' Nobody ever called her pretty. She stayed a while, and he was very friendly. He gave her a big tip when she left, but the housekeeper bawled her out for taking so long, and after a few months she was fired for being pregnant."

Qwilleran huffed into his moustache. It sounded like the scenario for an old silent movie. "Go on."

"She was afraid to go home to Ugley Gardens, so she slept in barns all summer and asked for food at farm-houses. She knew all about babies, because her mother had so many. Hers was born in a shack on Chipmunk Road. It was a boy. She called him Donald, but she couldn't keep him. She put him in a box and hoped and prayed somebody would find him. A policeman found him. Everybody was talking about the abandoned baby. They gave him another name, and she heard about him once in a while—her Donald."

"Then she continued to live in the area?"

"Yes sir, and she always knew what he was doing—playing football, working in the woods, working at the hotel, winning the gold medal."

"Does she know he's suspected of murder?"

"Yes, sir."

"If it's any comfort to . . . Betsy . . . let her know that the best lawyer in the county will handle his case."

"Thank you, sir. . . . What if—what if they find out Donald killed his own father? . . . He didn't know."

Qwilleran hesitated just long enough to swallow. "Of course he didn't."

"YOW!" came a piercing comment from the top of the refrigerator.

Qwilleran thanked her for the story, said he would consider it for the book, escorted her to the car in the barnyard.

"You told the story very well, Nora—in your own way. Do me one favor: Don't tell it to anyone else."

"Yes, sir."

He would not embarrass her by confronting her with the truth—that Betsy's story was really her own—but Nora knew that he knew; that was evident in the beseeching look in her eyes when she said, "Thank you, sir."

To Qwilleran, the incredible coincidence was Koko's persistent interest in *Oedipus Rex,* the ancient story of a king who unwittingly killed his own father.

After Nora left, Koko came down from the refrigerator with two hearty thumps, and Yum Yum floated down like a feather. They had a small reward for good behavior, while Qwilleran had a strong cup of coffee and read another Annie-Fanny letter. It was dated November 30.

Dear Fanny—

I wish I could write a cheerful letter as the holiday season approaches, but I'm worried about Dana, and I know you won't mind if I unload my troubles on you. My dear, adorable husband has just lost his job at the department store. He says they're cutting down the sales staff, but wait a minute! The Christmas rush has started, and they should be hiring extra salespeople, shouldn't they? I can't help wondering if he's been drinking on his lunch period or, even worse, on the job! I don't object to cocktails before dinner (although I've given them up until baby comes) but Dana has a tendency to drink a wee bit too much when he's unhappy. I can understand that he's frustrated by the lack of acting opportunities here, but the thought that he may have lied to me is most discouraging. I must not allow myself to get depressed. I must go on dreaming our dream: an acting career for Dana, a house in the suburbs, and a healthy baby! Dana is going to try for a job as a waiter, and I know he'll be a good one, because he has great charm and can play any role well, but I worry that he'd have even more opportunities to sneak a drink. Oh Fanny! Please think good thoughts!

Love from Annie

Qwilleran could empathize with the father-to-be. He, too, had succumbed to a drinking problem when faced with a stressful situation. And he could sympathize with the mother-to-be, faced with fears and responsibilities.

He kept reminding himself: This happened more than half a century ago . . . There's nothing I can do . . . Why am I so involved?

He read the letter dated December 29:

Dear Fanny—

This will be brief. Just want you to know that I'm really unwell. I've missed quite a few days at the library, and today the doctor told me to stay home and take care of myself or risk losing the baby.

Dana is working at a convenience store evenings, and I sit up waiting for him. When he comes home, he's had too much to drink. What can I do? How will it all end?

Love from Annie

Before Qwilleran could marshal his reactions, the telephone interrupted. Mildred was inviting him and Polly to dinner the following evening. "I know it's short notice," she said, "but I thought it would be neighborly to have a little dinner for Mr. Nightingale. Just an informal get-together, with cocktails and a casserole. Polly says he's absolutely charming! Are you free, Qwill?"

"I'm always free for one of your casseroles, Mildred, with or without a charming guest of honor."

Mildred could not hear him muttering to himself about Polly's discoveries: first the "charming" French-Canadian professor in Quebec City . . . and then the "charming" hand-kissing jeweler from Chicago . . . and now the "charming" rare book dealer from Boston.

"What time will you expect us?" he asked. "And what's for dessert?"

sixteen

Monday, September 21—*'Tis folly to kill the goose that lays the golden eggs.*

As Qwilleran tore off yesterday's page from Culvert McBee's calendar, he regretted that the month would soon end. On the last Tuesday he would devote his column to the ten-year-old's carefully researched collection of wise sayings. Some were old favorites; others had ambiguous meanings; a few were of foreign origin. All would be printed, having been stowed away in a kitchen drawer, and readers would be encouraged to discuss them over coffee at the Dimsdale Diner, tea at the Ittibittiwassee Estates, and beer at the Black Bear Café.

At two o'clock the *Moose County Something* was routinely delivered to the newspaper sleeve on Trevelyan Road, and Qwilleran strolled down the lane to pick it up. The carrier was late, however, so he went into the art center to kill time.

He found Thornton Haggis in the manager's office and

asked him, "What's that hearse doing in the parking lot?"
Actually it was a very long, very old black Cadillac.

"It's the Tibbitts' car. Rhoda's conducting a workshop in silhouette-cutting. Five women and one man are in the classroom, snipping away. Would you like to join them?"

"No, thanks. I'd rather learn how to turn wood. Your two wood-turnings are a big hit: the spalted elm vessel on the coffee table and the spalted maple box in the library. People like to touch them."

"Yes, they're sensuous—even sensual," Thornton said.

"My male cat is fascinated by the splotches on the spalted box. He sniffs them and touches them with his paw. I'd wanted to buy it, you know, but Mildred had already spoken for it. Did you know she was buying it for me?"

"In Moose County everyone knows what everyone is doing, Qwill. You should have learned that by now."

"Okay. This is a test question: Who is Kirt Nightingale?"

"You got me! Who is he?"

"A rare book dealer who claims to have come from this area."

"Well," said the stonecutter, "I never cut a headstone for a Nightingale, and I went through all the old ledgers of the monument works when I wrote that paper for the historical society. There were Wrens and Crowes, but no Nightingales."

Qwilleran looked out the window. "There's the newspaper carrier. He's late today."

Thornton walked with him to the door. "Anything new about the hijacking?"

"I believe not."

"Everett, my youngest son, knew Boze Campbell when they both had summer jobs with a forestry outfit. In camp they'd sit around telling jokes and drinking beer, but Boze just sat there whittling and chewing gum. His jack-knife was a treasured possession. He'd start with a tree limb and whittle it down to the size of a pencil."

When Qwilleran left the center, he saw a penny alongside the front path. He left it there, certain that it was one of Mildred's calculated penny-drops. He now had four lucky pennies in the spalted maple box— all grimy, tarnished, weatherworn examples of genuine lost pennies.

It was too early to dress for dinner and too late to start another serious project, so he sat in a comfortable chair and leafed through the latest newsmagazine. In the large empty silence of the barn the only sound was the turning of pages, until . . . His ear was alert to cat noises, and he heard a special kind of mumbling. Yum Yum never mumbled. It was obviously Koko, talking to himself as he undertook a difficult task. Qwilleran was out of his chair in a flash.

The foyer was the scene of Koko's investigation. He lay on his left side on the flagstone floor, and extended a long left foreleg under the rug; then he withdrew it and rolled over to stretch the other foreleg under the Oriental—which happened to be very thin, very old, and very valuable. Yum Yum watched with interest from a nearby table; Qwilleran watched with admiration Koko's diligence and perseverance. The determined animal now tried a frontal attack, flattening himself on his belly and squirming under the carpet nose-first like a snake. His ears disappeared, then his forelegs, then half of his long torso. When he finally backed out, he had a treasure clamped in his mouth.

It was a foil gum-wrapper! Barry Morghan had dropped it into the Chinese water bucket two weeks before. It was Yum Yum's hobby to scour wastebaskets for collectibles to store in secret places, and this was probably the first gum-wrapper she had ever seen. Why did she want it now? Did Koko know she wanted it? How did he know she wanted it? If he knew, would he be likely to do her a favor? Did cats do favors for other cats?

Questions about cat behavior have no answers, Qwilleran decided. He gave them an early dinner and had time for one more letter before leaving for the Riker party. Date: January 1:

Dear Fanny—

Happy New Year! And thank you so much for your generous check. I thought Dana would be pleased with the thoughtful Christmas gift, but for some strange reason he was angry. Then I said it was a loan, to be repaid after the baby comes, but he raved and ranted. He'd been drinking and was really out of control. He tore up the check and said he wasn't going to accept charity from his wife's girlfriend. Oh, dear! What to do? Sometimes I'm at my wit's end! One minute he's wonderful, and after a drink he's not the same person. His masculine pride is hurt because he can't support us. Yesterday he was yelling, "I'll support my wife and child even if I have to work the garbage trucks or hold up gas stations!" That's when he tore up your check. And today he was hung over and filled with remorse. Then he gets suicidal. Today I screamed at him, "Don't talk like that in front of our baby!" I've never screamed at anyone in my life! Have you ever heard me scream, Fanny? I don't know what's happening to me.

Love from Annie

Qwilleran threw the letter back in the box. There was something naggingly familiar about the scene Annie had described.

On the way to Indian Village to meet Polly's "charming" antiquarian, he stopped at the Mackintosh Inn to have another look at Lady Anne—so serene, so poised. That was the way he remembered her. A few minutes later he was at The Willows, greeting Polly, also poised and serene.

They walked to The Birches. He was carrying a bottle of wine and yellow mums for their hosts; she had a jar of honey tied with a ribbon for the guest of honor.

"It's the traditional house-warming gift," she explained. "Do you know the line, Qwill, about *honey and plenty of money* from Edward Lear? Kirt has a book of Lear's nonsense poems that's valued at twelve thousand. We were talking about it yesterday."

"Has he moved in?" Qwilleran asked.

"No. The moving van arrives tomorrow."

When they arrived at the Riker condo, the vehicle with Massachusetts tags was parked in the visitor's slot.

"Isn't that an exciting car?" Polly cried. It was a Jaguar.

They presented their gifts, Polly saying to the book dealer, "Here's to honey and lots of money!"

He was introduced as Kirtwell Nightingale but said he liked to be called Kirt. Qwilleran sized him up as an ordinary-looking man of ordinary build, with ordinary clothing and haircut and handshake.

Cocktails were served, and Arch proposed a toast. "In your garden of life may your pea pods never be empty!"

Qwilleran asked, "What brings you to Little Arctica, Kirt?"

"I grew up around here," the man said, "and at a certain age one has a yearning to come home."

"Did you live in Pickax?"

"No. Out in the country." He's evasive, Qwilleran thought; probably grew up in Mudville or Ugley Gardens.

Mildred said, "Qwill has a fabulous collection of old books in his barn."

"An accumulation, not a collection," he corrected her. "I simply wander into Eddington Smith's place and buy something I'd like to read, or something I've read before and never owned."

"Not all collectors buy for investment," the dealer said. "Many buy for personal reading pleasure. My only advice is to check the book's condition. It should have a secure binding and all its pages, with no tears or underlining—and of course a clean cover."

Qwilleran asked, "What if your cat has a hobby of knocking books off the shelf?"

"You have a problem."

Polly's question was: "If I want to collect books, how do I start?"

"First decide whether you want to be a generalist or a specialist. It's my humble opinion that specialists have more fun. If you focus on one category—zoology, ship-wrecks, or Thomas Edison, for example—the hunt can be exciting."

Polly said she would choose ornithology; Mildred, old cookbooks; Arch, life in early America.

Qwilleran said, "I have an old copy of *Domestic Manners of the Americans* that you can have for twenty bucks."

"Sure. You bought it for three."

"Qwill," said Kirt, "you're on your way to becoming an antiquarian bookseller. All it takes is one profitable sale, and you get the fever . . . and by the way, Polly gave me some back copies of your column. You're a splendid writer! And she tells me that's a portrait of your mother in the lobby of the inn. A handsome woman!"

Mildred interrupted by announcing dinner: individual casseroles of shrimp and asparagus, green salad with toasted sesame seeds and Stilton cheese, and cranberry parfaits.

On the way home Polly asked Qwilleran what he thought of their new neighbor.

"Not a bad guy!" he said.

It was midnight when the brown van drove into the barnyard, and Qwilleran expected a scolding. Instead, Koko and Yum Yum staged a demonstration in the foyer—prowling back and forth and jumping at the two tall windows that flanked the double doors. Qwilleran floodlighted that side of the building, expecting to see a marauding raccoon. There was no sign of wildlife, but shadowy movement could be seen behind the screens of the gazebo.

A prowler, he thought. Boze Campbell!

Before he could call the police, however, a thin figure materialized out of the shadows and came running toward the barn with waving arms and shouts of "Mr. Q! Mr. Q!"

"Lenny!" Qwilleran shouted back, going out to meet him. "What are you doing here? You're supposed to be in Duluth!"

"I came back. Do you have any food? I'm starved. I spent my last nickel on breakfast."

"How did you get here? Where's your truck?"

"Out of gas on the highway. I walked the rest of the way."

"Come in! Come in! I'll make a ham and cheese sandwich. What would you like to drink? Beer? Coffee? Cola?"

"Milk, if you've got it."

Qwilleran put a glass and a plastic jug of milk on the snack bar. "Help yourself while I throw the sandwich together. Mustard? Horseradish?"

"Both."

"Is rye bread okay?"

"Anything." Lenny gulped a glassful and poured another.

"Do you know what's been going on here since you left? The stolen pistol? The hijacking?"

"Everything," the young man said. "Mom phoned my aunt's house every night."

"Why did you decide to come home?"

"I'm worried about Boze. I'm afraid he'll get himself shot. Some trigger-happy clod will see him in the woods and panic. He'll think he's shooting him in self-defense."

"So you think he's hiding out in the woods," Qwilleran said. "That's my hunch, too, although it's generally thought he'll steal another vehicle and disappear Down Below. . . . Here, try this sandwich. I have ice cream in the freezer, too. Don't talk until you finish eating." Sitting on a bar stool Qwilleran filled him in with the latest news: "Osmond Hasselrich died . . . The Mark Twain Festival is postponed . . . Amanda Goodwinter is running for mayor . . . Homer Tibbitt celebrated his ninety-eighth . . . The Sloans are selling their drugstore and moving to Florida."

Lenny chewed in silence, obviously more interested in his own crisis than in local news. After he had devoured a chocolate sundae, the two of them went to the library area and stretched out in lounge chairs.

Qwilleran said, "Tell me what you propose to do."

"Get him out of the woods for his own safety. Under normal conditions he could live off the land. He has his jackknife, and now he has a gun, and he has friends out there in backwoods stores who'd sell him ammo and matches and flashlight batteries and chewing gum. They'd even help to hide him. They're on his side. He's their own kind. Besides, he's a hero."

"Do you think you can get him to come out of the woods and give himself up?"

"He trusted me, or he wouldn't have told me what

happened. Now maybe he thinks I'm a double-crosser, but that's a chance I've got to take. Mr. Barter told me that no Moose County jury would convict a simple country boy duped by a big-city sharpie. I knew she wasn't that guy's niece! I've been working in hotels since I was sixteen, and I know a bimbo when I see one. She tried to come on to me at the desk, you know, but I wasn't having any. If only I could have guessed . . . She'd be in jail, and the old guy would be alive, and Boze would still be a hero."

Qwilleran stroked his moustache. "What makes you think you can find him?"

"I'm pretty sure I know where he is," said Lenny, looking wise. "If we can take your van—"

"Wait a minute, Lenny. Are you expecting me to go out there?"

"We gotta."

Qwilleran considered it a hare-brained mission, although his professional curiosity and sense of adventure were undermining his better judgment. He hesitated.

"Do you have a couple of flashlights?" Lenny asked.

They drove out Chipmunk Road—in silence until Qwilleran said, "You mentioned that Boze could buy chewing gum from backwoods stores."

"Yeah, he's a chain-chewer. Always has a wad in his mouth. At the inn, where gum-chewing isn't allowed on the job, the housekeeper found gum-wrappers in the wastebasket behind the desk . . . and wads of gum stuck under the edge of the counter. It was my job to straighten him out. Not easy."

"The midnight shift must be dull. What does the night

clerk do to pass the time—when he isn't talking to bimbos?"

"On the six-to-midnight I get a chance to study. Boze liked comic books. . . . All that seems like a long time ago. I've lived a year in the past week."

After a while Qwilleran asked, "Isn't this the way to the Big B mine?"

"Yep."

"It was once owned and operated by a woman."

"Oh?"

Lenny's mind was somewhere else—not on the conversation—until the Big B shafthouse came in view, silvery in the moonlight.

"Take the next right," he said. "It's a dirt road."

It paralleled the six-foot chain-link fence that marked the limits of the mine property. Like all other mines the Big B was posted as dangerous, and the fence was topped with three courses of barbed wire.

"Okay, Mr. Q. Stop here. Let's get out and walk."

They took the flashlights. Although the moon was bright, the rutted lane was shaded by overhanging tree branches. The leaves had not yet begun to fall. As they walked, all was quiet except for the whine of tires on Chipmunk Road behind them—and the occasional scurrying of a small animal in the underbrush. At the northeast corner of the fenced site the lane turned south and became even more primitive.

Lenny said in a hushed voice, "Boze and I used to play around here when we were kids. We knew how to get over the barbed wire without skinning a knee and how to pry a board loose from the shafthouse."

"You mean you went inside that dilapidated wreck?"

"Crazy, wasn't it? It was spooky inside—all scaffolding and ladders. We could hear the water sloshing in the mineshaft a zillion feet below. There's a subterranean lake down there."

"How do you know?"

"Everybody says so. All I know is, we threw pebbles down and heard them splash. We'd climb to the top platform with a pocketful of pebbles and sit there and eat a candy bar."

"Didn't you realize how dangerous it was? Those timbers are more than a century old."

"Yeah, but fourteen inches square and put together with handmade spikes a foot long! We climbed around like monkeys. We were only nine years old. Our only fear was that Mom would find out. Once we were dumb enough to try smoking on the top platform. Boze had stolen a cigarette somewhere, and I had book matches. We lit it all right, but it didn't taste as good as a candy bar. We dropped it down the shaft and heard it fizzle out in the water—or imagined we did. That was one of our finer moments."

"I'll bet," Qwilleran said, thinking what a sheltered life he and Arch had lived in Chicago.

"Sh-h-h!" Lenny flashed his light on the ground. "He's here! There's a gum-wrapper!" A scrap of foil caught the light.

Qwilleran's moustache twitched as he remembered Koko's obsession with the bit of foil under the rug.

"Look, Mr. Q! Here's where he built a campfire!" There was a charred circle on the ground and some small bones. "He cooked a rabbit! I'll bet he's saving the skins to make a blanket!"

Qwilleran looked around uneasily. He felt they were being watched through a knothole in old boards. He could see a pinpoint of light inside. "Let's get out of here," he whispered.

But Lenny began to shout. "Boze! It's Lenny! Are you all right? We came to help you!"

There was no answer.

"I know he's in there," Lenny whispered. "I can see pinpoints of light. Flashlight. Or lantern."

"This is insane!" Qwilleran hissed.

Lenny shouted again. "Boze! Everything's gonna be all right! Mr. Q's here! He's gonna help you!"

All was quiet again, and then they heard a gunshot from the tower. Qwilleran grabbed Lenny's upper arm roughly and propelled him back along the primitive road.

There was another shot . . . then sounds of thumping and crashing and splintering of old wood . . . a splash . . . and silence again.

Breathless and wordless, they hurried along the dirt lane leading to the highway. In the van Qwilleran phoned 911 and backed the vehicle out to the shoulder of Chipmunk Road. They waited, with headlights beamed on the shafthouse. Lenny sat quietly, shivering.

"Need a sweater?" Qwilleran asked. "There's one on the back seat. . . . When the police come, let me do the talking."

One by one the emergency vehicles appeared: the sheriff's patrol car, an ambulance, the Pickax police, the rescue squad. Qwilleran's presence lent credibility and seriousness to the incident. Not only did he have a press card; he was Mr. Q. As he reported it, they had been driving past and saw flickers of light in the tower—barely visible in the chinks between the weathered boards. They drove into the lane for a closer look, heard gunshots, and backed out in a hurry.

Leaving the scene and heading back to Pickax, he said to his passenger, "Do you want to be dropped at Lois's house? How will you reach your truck in the morning? Is there anything I can do? Let me give you some money for gas. Better not give Lois any of the details."

Lenny was in a fog. He just wanted to go home. He had lost a brother. He felt guilty. His intentions had been good. He should have stayed in Duluth. He should have left everything to fate. He was jinxed.

Qwilleran listened sympathetically, murmuring remonstrance, encouragement, condolences—whatever was needed.

seventeen

TUESDAY, SEPTEMBER 22—*Can a leopard change his spots?*

After the late-hours episode at the Big B mine, Qwilleran wanted to sleep late, but the Siamese had other ideas. They howled outside his door at twenty-minute intervals and were suspiciously quiet in between. When he shuffled down the ramp to investigate, he found that someone had pried open a kitchen drawer . . . and someone had removed the twenty-one previous pages torn from Culvert's calendar . . . and someone had distributed them throughout the main floor. He presumed it to be a collaboration—what he called their Mungojerrie-Rumpelteazer act—and he collected the litter of paper with grudging admiration: They knew how to capture a person's attention!

During the morning he avoided news bulletins on WPKX, preferring to wait for the two o'clock edition of the *Moose County Something*. Meanwhile, he delivered a vanload of books and personal belongings to his condo—

Unit Four at The Willows. A moving van from Boston was unloading at Unit Two, and the Jaguar was parked under the visitors' carport.

On the way back to town it occurred to him that now might be a good time to present Polly with a gift he had special-ordered and was saving for Sweetest Day. Now he reasoned, however, that his move back to Indian Village had a celebratory aspect, and in midday he walked into her office with a gift-wrapped package.

She was having a vegetarian lunch at her desk. "Have some celery straws," she invited slyly, knowing he despised them. Then she saw the small box in gilt paper and ribbons. "For me? What's the occasion, Qwill?"

"It's Tuesday," he said with characteristic calm.

After fumbling excitedly with the wrappings, she uncovered an octagonal bottle of French perfume encased in gold filligree. She was stunned! She tripped over her words—had never seen such a beautiful bottle—had never dreamed she'd have such a famous scent to spray on her skin.

Both of them were remembering an evening last month, between sunset and dark, when twilight descended on the world like a blue mist and brought a magical silence—l'heure bleue.

"Glad you like it," Qwilleran said. He grabbed a handful of celery straws.

Pickax commercial establishments and government agencies no longer observed the quaint custom of shutting down for lunch between twelve and one, but it was still wise to avoid that hour for making transactions. Qwilleran went home to give the cats their midday treat and to start cleaning out the refrigerator for his own lunch. Celia's catered specialties that he had been stockpiling in the freezer would be transported to winter quarters in dry ice.

He had a list of individuals to notify about his move. It was only a gesture—to the bank manager, postmaster, garage owner, bookseller, and so forth. The truth was that everyone in town knew where Mr. Q was living at any given time, but it was a compliment to be on his list.

Foremost was the chief of police. His department always kept an eye on the barn when Qwilleran was not in residence.

"Andy, tonight's your last chance to drop in for a nightcap," Qwilleran said to the disgruntled officer sitting at the computer. Brodie was always irked and impatient when confronted with the contraption that he loathed.

"Be there at ten o'clock," the chief said brusquely. "Can't stay long."

At two o'clock the *Moose County Something* reached the newsstands with the headline

SUSPECT DIES IN MINESHAFT

A fugitive from the law fell to his death in the shaft of the abandoned Big B mine early this morning. John Campbell, who was wanted for murder and two counts of theft, was hiding out in the shafthouse when an unidentified motorist noticed a light in the tower and called 911 after hearing a gunshot.

The sheriff's department, Pickax police and rescue squad personnel responded.

The suspect, known locally as Boze Campbell, had won a gold medal for a perfect three-out-of-three caber-toss in the Highland Games earlier this month, before disappearing into the woods, assaulting a deputy, stealing her revolver and hijacking the city's bookmobile.

He was 25, a native of Moose County with no known parentage, a student at MCCC, and a part-time employee of the Mackintosh Inn. He leaves no survivors.

A sidebar on the same page was headed

BOZE MOURNED BY SPORT FANS

When news of John (Boze) Campbell's death became known, sport fans gathered at Lois's Luncheonette to grieve, extol his athletic feats, praise his woodsmanship, and refuse to believe he was guilty of crimes.

Lois Inchpot, who had known him since he was a young boy, said, "He was a nice young man—kind of sweet—but he'd had no bringing up, and my son Lenny and I sort of adopted him. He didn't drink or smoke, and he loved the woods. When he won the gold medal, I felt like my own son had won it. We're gonna have a nice funeral for him, and my customers are taking up a collection to buy him a headstone. I hope they find the real murderer. I know Boze couldn't have done it."

After reading this, Qwilleran was hardly surprised to hear from Lenny, phoning from the kitchen of the lunchroom, against a clatter of pots and pans and his mother's shouted commands.

"Did you read it?" Lenny asked abruptly.

"Yes. Your mother's statement was very touching. She's a good-hearted woman, Lenny."

"They didn't tell how Boze was tricked into doing it!"

"The paper printed information released by the police. Use your common sense! Don't you suppose the authorities are on the trail of the woman who duped him? She's done it before! She's a menace! Sit tight, and see what they discover."

"There's another thing, Mr. Q. When we heard the gunshot last night, I thought Boze had shot himself, but today . . . I'm wondering if . . . he tripped and fell and the gun went off accidentally. What do you think?"

"Good question. We'll never know, will we? Whatever makes you comfortable in your mind, it seems to me, that's what you should believe."

Qwilleran was struggling with questions of his own—about Koko's recent behavior. All cats, he knew, are psychic to a degree, but Koko, who had more than the normal number of whiskers, was exceptionally prescient. It was his system of communication that baffled one.

He howled in the night. He knocked books off the shelf. He tossed pencils around like Boze tossing the caber. He licked photographs. He dug up clues and hid others.

Who could say how much was pertinent evidence and how much was catly playfulness? And how much was strictly coincidence?

When Koko pilfered Brazil nuts from the nut bowl, did his actions have anything to do with a cruel trick played on Boze Campbell? Or had he found something deliciously oily into which he could sink his fangs?

Qwilleran would have liked a confidant with whom to discuss such arcane matters, but even his close friends were unreceptive. The least likely candidate happened to be the best prospect, and he was coming to the barn for a drink at ten o'clock. Chief Andrew Brodie had scoffed at Qwilleran's "smart cat" at the beginning, but he was gradually coming around.

In the evening the temperature dropped and a west wind arose. Qwilleran put on a wool turtleneck jersey and a heavy sweater and built a fire in the library fireplace. The barn was drafty; it was high time to move.

The Siamese, whose hair was standing on end, took up positions on the hearth rug facing the blaze, as if to toast their whiskers. Qwilleran stretched out in the lounge chair closest to the fire and wondered if Andy would prefer a hot buttered rum to his usual scotch.

Meanwhile, he read another Annie-Fanny letter, dated January 3:

Dear Fanny—
    The worst has happened! Yesterday I was sitting alone, reading Spenser's *Faerie Queene* to take my

mind off the new year. We had neither the money nor the spirit to celebrate. Dana had been trying to get a job as a waiter, but the restaurants were hiring only experienced help. Finally he lied—and was hired. But he didn't last more than one shift. It was too obvious that he had never worked in a restaurant before. When he came home he was feeling positively suicidal. I was really worried, because I knew his brother had taken his own life. . . . But yesterday he went out again to look for work. I felt so sorry for him, I thought my heart would break. But then I remembered my responsibility to my baby and started reading about the knight and ladies of old. Suddenly there was a knock on my door, and two police officers were there. They said, "Ma'am, we regret to inform you that your husband has been killed." I almost fainted, and they helped me to a chair. All I could think was: He's thrown himself in front of a bus! I managed to ask, "Was it a car accident?" They said, "No, ma'am. He was shot by a security guard during an attempted bank robbery . . ."

Qwilleran had read enough. He jumped up and threw the letter into the fireplace. "The past is dead!" he muttered, and he emptied the entire box of Klingenschoen correspondence into the blaze. A car pulled into the barnyard, and the cats pricked their ears, but Qwilleran had the poker and was feeding the flames.

Brodie let himself in and swaggered through the kitchen to the library. "It's a good night for a fire," he said in his commanding voice. "Temperature dropped twenty degrees since sundown. What are you doing? Burning vital evidence?"

"Getting rid of obsolete documents before I move. . . . Sit by the fire, Andy. How'd you like your scotch on a night like this?"

"Just a splash of tap water. Not too big a splash." He settled into a deep-cushioned armchair. "Don't let me get too comfortable and forget to pick up my wife at ten o'clock. She's at the church helping to mend winter clothing they collected for the needy. She's been there since four o'clock. They serve the women supper."

"What did you do for food?"

"Aw, I found some beans and franks in the fridge and warmed them up."

"Sounds better than what I had." Qwilleran served the beverages and individual bowls of nuts—the luxury mix. "Keep your eye on the Brazil nuts, Andy. Koko collects them. Doesn't eat them, just collects them."

"So you're moving back to the Village! Anything new out there?"

"A new neighbor, Kirtwell Nightingale. Know him? Says he's from around here, although he's been living in Boston."

"Never heard of a Nightingale in these parts, and I worked for the sheriff's department long enough to memorize the county book. The name sounds phony to me."

"He sells rare books from his home, some priced in five figures."

"Hmmm," said the chief. "Sounds a bit shady. Better keep an eye on him. Put your smart cat on his tail."

Then he spotted Kiltie on the bar. "What's that strange-looking thing?"

"A vintage mechanical bank, about 1930, from the Sprenkle collection." Qwilleran brought it into the circle around the fire, extorted a dime from his guest and pressed the lever. Brodie laughed with gusto when the canny Scot blinked and pocketed the coin.

"And have you seen Thornton Haggis's woodturnings?" Qwilleran put the spalted maple box on the table at his guest's elbow. "Pick it up. Examine it. See how perfectly the lid fits."

Brodie looked inside. "Pennies!"

"I'm saving up to buy a yacht," Qwilleran said. "Didn't you ever pick up a lucky penny in the street, Andy?"

"Not since I was six years old."

Nothing was said about Boze Campbell until the chief had downed his second drink. Then he asked abruptly. "What were you doing at the Big B mine last night?"

"Driving in from a party in the country. It's a sad ending to a sad story. Who should know better than you?"

"It's not over till it's over. Off the record, there'll be a break in the case soon—real soon. The FBI is watching the girl. She's pulled other scams with a variety of aliases."

At that moment Koko, who was sitting on the hearth rug, rose in the air and landed on the end table. He gave Brodie an impudent stare, nipped the knob of the maple box, yowled, and jumped to the floor.

"What's wrong with him?" the chief asked.

"He does some peculiar things, but he usually has a reason," Qwilleran explained. "Remember hearing about the paper towels he draped around the kitchen? You had just discovered that all the towels in Delacamp's suite were missing. What happened?"

"Well . . . this is just between you and me . . . when we finally unlocked the jewel cases, they were empty! She had cleaned them out before checking them into the manager's safe that night. And it's our theory that she wrapped the jewels in towels and had them in duffel bags when Boze drove her to the airport. All her regular luggage and clothes were left in her room."

Qwilleran asked seriously, "Would you say that Koko's demonstration with the paper towels was only a coincidence?" He was thinking about Brazil nuts, snapshot-licking and the gum-wrapper.

"Couple of years ago I'd have said yes. When I met Lieutenant Hames that time Down Below and he told me about your smart cat, I didn't believe a word. Hames is a great cop but a little nuts, you know. . . . But now—" He jumped up. "It's almost ten! Thanks for the drinks. Tell Koko he'll be sworn in next week. If the sheriff can have a dog, the PPD can have a cat on the force."

He was striding for the exit, and Qwilleran was following.

Brodie was saying, "If you ever get married, Qwill, never be late in picking up your wife. We're a one-car family, now that we can't use official vehicles when off-duty."

Qwilleran consulted his watch. "You have two minutes to get to the church. You can make it, if you drive the wrong way around the Park Circle. Too bad you don't have a siren."

Brodie slid behind the wheel and said, just before driving away, "Stick close to your radio, I think there'll be news."

Qwilleran stirred the fire and added another log, which the Siamese appreciated. In removing the refreshment tray he noted that his guest had not touched the Brazil nuts—and neither had Koko. That meant that the case was closed, as far as the cat was concerned. He had lost interest in the yellow pencils, *Oedipus Rex*, and snapshots of the Highland Games. To Qwilleran that was proof that these were messages and not mere cat-play.

Sprawling in front of the fire he thought about other things and dozed lightly until a dull ache in the center of his forehead roused him. Koko was sitting on the arm of the chair, staring at him. He sat up, and Koko scampered to the feeding station in the kitchen. It was almost eleven o'clock: time for the news, time for the bedtime snack. While the cats bent over their crunchy treat, Qwilleran heard the WPKX announcer say:

"A woman alleged to have planned the robbery and murder of a Chicago jeweler in Pickax has been arrested as she boarded a plane for Rio de Janeiro, carrying large quantities of jewelry and cash. She had registered at the Mackintosh Inn as Pamela North and was posing as the victim's niece and assistant. Investigators say she tricked a local man, John (Boze) Campbell, into committing the crime. Using a number of other aliases, she has perpetrated similar schemes elsewhere. Her legal name is now known to be Harriet Marie Penney. Campbell fell to his death early this morning in the shafthouse of the Big B mine, where he was in hiding."

"Penney?... *Penney?*" Qwilleran exclaimed. "Koko, did you hear that?"

"Yargle," Koko said between a yowl and a swallow.